SWEET BEGINNINGS

A little hope changes everything...

Artist Hope Ryan dreams of seeing her artwork displayed in top galleries again, but a devastating betrayal left her unable to paint as she once did. Instead, she settles for creating unique items for tourists and wedding couples in her hometown. Although Hope longs for more, she refuses to venture outside her comfort zone, fearing the heartbreak and disappointment of failing again.

Highly paid sportscaster Josh Cooper never overcame his bitterness after an injury on the football field sidelined him for good. Finding his solace in alcohol and women only made matters worse until he finally hit rock bottom. Now, he's looking for redemption. When he's asked to fly a wedding gown across the country for one of the victims of his wrongs, he doesn't hesitate.

Arriving in Indigo Bay, Josh finds himself captivated by the artist creating the wedding favors. He knows exactly what he wants—Hope—even though she deserves someone better. Can Josh prove he's more than a broken has-been? Or · but also lose himself?

D1484446

INDIGO BAY SWEET ROMANCE SERIES

What is the Indigo Bay Sweet Romance Series? It's tons of fun for readers! But more specifically, it is a set of books written by authors who love romance. Grab a glass of sweet tea, sit on the porch, and get ready to be swept away into this charming South Carolina beach town.

The Indigo Bay world has been written so readers can dive in anywhere in the series without missing a beat. Read one or all–they're sweet, fun rides that you won't soon forget. Also, as a special treat, you'll see some recurring characters. How many can *you* find?

Sweet Beginnings

Indigo Bay Sweet Romance Series

Melissa McClone

Sweet Beginnings
Indigo Bay Sweet Romance Series (Book 8)

Copyright © 2018 Melissa McClone

Cover by Najla Qamber Designs
www.najlaqamberdesigns.com

Cardinal Press, LLC
May 2018
ISBN-13: 978-1-944777-06-7

For those who haven't given up even when it seemed impossible to keep going.

1

On an overcast day in May, Josh Cooper stood at Jenny Hanford's front door. He kept his arms pressed against his sides rather than raising his hand to the doorbell. He might be thirty-two and a well-known football commentator, but he felt more like a fourteen-year-old high school freshman with zero confidence.

Forget being nervous. He'd passed that stage two hours ago, and he was on the verge of losing it.

Your fault.

That didn't make being here easier.

The pounding of his heart sounded like a death knell. Not surprising given he hadn't spoken to Jenny Hanford, a former classmate from Berry Lake High School, since their epic disaster of a first, and last, date at Brew & Steep, a local coffee shop, in July.

You have the right to remain silent…

Being arrested for disorderly conduct seemed like forever ago, but only ten months had passed. Ten months that had seen Jenny's life change. Ten months of trying to keep himself from losing… everything.

Stop procrastinating.

Even though Josh wanted to be anywhere—other than in jail—but here, he jabbed the doorbell.

Chimes sounded. Not a typical ding-dong like most of the other houses in Berry Lake, Washington. Jenny's was ten times nicer than the typical homes in the area. With her books hitting the bestseller lists and her series being turned into a movie franchise, she could afford a bigger estate on the outskirts of town.

The seconds ticked by. Maybe Jenny wasn't home.

The thought brought instant relief. He wanted—needed—a reprieve, even if he *had* to do this eventually.

The door opened. Missy Hanford, Jenny's sister-in-law, grimaced. "What are you doing here?"

Josh understood the harsh expression and the frustrated tone. He'd gone from being Berry Lake's golden boy to persona non grata. To be honest, he deserved the hatred and lack of respect. Both were better than people's pity for being…

A drunk.

He took a breath. "I want to speak with Jenny."

"She's writing." Missy gripped the doorknob hard enough her knuckles turned white. "I don't want to disturb her."

Missy's reluctance made sense. She'd been the one to give him Jenny's phone number and convince her homebody sister-in-law to meet him for coffee.

"I'm sorry I put you in a rough spot last summer. I never meant…" He shifted his weight between his feet. "I tried to stay sober before meeting Jenny."

But like most days, he'd failed. Only he hadn't failed in such a spectacular or public manner until that ill-fated date with Jenny—aka bestselling thriller author Jenna Ford.

He tucked the tops of his fingers into his pant pockets. "I'm here to apologize. It won't take long. Please. This is important."

He must have sounded pathetic or desperate because Missy's gaze softened. It gave him hope she wouldn't slam the door in his face, anyway.

"I'll see if Jenny's available," Missy said. "You can wait in the living room."

Blowing out a breath, Josh stepped inside. The scent of fresh-baked cookies surrounded him, reminding him of… home.

The house he'd purchased last summer when he'd returned to Berry Lake was nothing but a shell, a place to store boxes full of his stuff and a few pieces of furniture. It was also where he kept his plane in a hangar by the airstrip out back. He hadn't spent a night there in months. No reason to unpack and create a life for himself in his hometown when he wasn't sure what might happen.

Missy closed the door. "Don't touch anything."

He held up his hands. "I won't."

A visit to the drunk tank was enough to stop him from doing anything illegal, including driving over the speed limit. Paranoid, maybe, but that had been one of the worst days of his life. At least until he'd entered rehab.

As Missy walked out, he stared at the bookshelf full of hardcover novels written under Jenny's pseudonym. The pretty bookworm who'd gotten straight As through high school was now more famous than him. That was one reason he'd asked her out when he arrived in town—he thought they would be Berry Lake's perfect celebrity couple. Maybe if his best friend hadn't been a bottle of whiskey that might have happened, but he'd lost his shot. She was engaged to someone else now.

You have only yourself to blame.

His insides twisted with a mix of fear and unease—what Josh felt whenever he saw someone he'd wronged with his drinking. He was on his "making amends" portion of his recovery; he'd been visiting each name on his list. Jenny was the last one.

"Hey, Josh." Jenny entered the living room. She wore jeans, a long-sleeved T-shirt, and fuzzy polka-dotted socks. Her long, caramel-blonde hair was pulled into a loose ponytail. No makeup on her face, but she didn't need any. Never had. A diamond engagement ring sparkled on her left ring finger.

"Hi." He swallowed around the lump in his throat. "Thanks for seeing me."

"I have to admit you're the last person I expected to drop by today." She sounded surprised, not annoyed.

A good sign? He hoped so.

"I should have let you know I was coming by." He hadn't called or texted in case she'd blocked his number. That would have made being here harder. "To be honest, I was afraid you might not want to talk to me."

"Missy said it was important." Jenny hadn't said she'd wanted to talk, but Josh understood.

"I…" Words failed him. He stared at his shoes.

Jenny took hold of his hand, led him to the couch, and motioned for him to sit. She sat next to him as if that was the most natural thing in the world to do.

"We might not have been friends or ran in the same crowd in high school, but I've known you my entire life. I've thought about you so many times over the past months." Jenny didn't appear upset, more… reserved, but she'd always been quiet. "How are you doing?"

Josh half-laughed, a nervous reaction. "That's a loaded question, though I'm sure whatever gossip you've heard isn't too far from the truth."

"I stay in my writing cave unless my fiancé is in town. I've only heard what Missy tells me. The gossip hasn't been that bad."

5

"Then someone is sugarcoating what happened to me." He tried to keep his tone lighthearted, but he didn't think he succeeded. "After my arrest, I went into rehab."

His third stay.

He'd signed himself out the first two times.

There wouldn't be a fourth. He'd committed himself to staying sober. Otherwise, he wouldn't be here today.

"It was a ninety-day residential program," he added. "Those supposedly have better success rates than the shorter ones. After that, I spent three months in a sober house. Now I'm staying with my folks."

Compassion filled her eyes. "Sounds like you're doing all you can."

He nodded once. "Before I forget, congrats on your engagement. I heard you're marrying an Army Ranger who found your message in a bottle, and that you nursed him back to health after a helicopter accident."

"Right on all accounts. The wedding is in mid-June." She grinned. "Guess we're both the topic of gossip in town. The price of fame."

"Or infamy, in my case."

She squeezed his hand—the gesture tightened the imaginary steel bands around his chest. "Your past won't always define you."

"I hope not." The emotion in those three words surprised him. Only his family, his therapist, Dr.

Kettering, and his sponsor, Rudy, knew the effort Josh was putting into his recovery. He'd never worked this hard at anything. Not even when he played football. "I haven't had a drink since that day we met at Brew & Steep."

The tension in her shoulders lessened, but surprise shone in her eyes. "That's great, Josh."

Some days didn't feel so great, not when he craved alcohol so badly he had to work out until it passed. He would not give up. He couldn't. On the flip side, he was in better shape now than when he played professionally.

"I stopped by to see you for two reasons." *Keep talking. You've done this before.* "First, I want to apologize for my behavior at the coffee shop. My drinking problem became yours."

Her gaze remained on him, but her fingers flexed. He hated upsetting her, but he needed to do this for both their sakes.

"I should have never posted that selfie of us on Instagram as if we were a couple, tried to get you to have sex with me, and picked a fight with that barista who wanted to help you get away from me."

Jenny clasped her hands on her lap. Her body tensed.

He wished she would hold his hand again, so he didn't feel so alone.

Stop procrastinating.

"This is uncomfortable to talk about, but that's

nothing compared to what I put you through. I'm sorry." He took a breath. "Truly sorry."

An apology wasn't enough for what he'd done, but he wanted to do this in steps. He'd learned to go slowly after more than one person hadn't cared what he'd had to say.

Would Jenny be like that?

He wouldn't blame her if she were, but so far, she'd been more understanding than others by not keeping her distance.

"Coming here and saying those words takes courage. I've tried to forget that day, but I haven't stopped hoping you'd get the help you needed. I'm happy you have. And proud of you." The sincerity in her voice matched the look in her eyes. "Apology accepted."

He blew out the breath he'd been holding. "Thanks."

"I'm sure the past ten months have been difficult."

Not trusting his voice, he nodded.

She smiled softly. "It's good you're in Berry Lake with family and friends around to support you."

If only…

His life had revolved around drinking. He was embarrassed to admit how much alcohol had clouded his judgment in everything from friendships to women.

"My recovery has shown me who my real friends are." Many people had deserted him, not only in his hometown but all over the country. Sober Josh wasn't as fun or generous with his money as drunk Josh. But he wasn't the victim here. Just a hot mess. "My family keeps me going."

"You're lucky to have them."

Nodding, he remembered Jenny's only family was her sister-in-law, Missy. Her parents had died following a car accident. Rob, her younger brother who was a Marine, had been killed while deployed.

Josh wouldn't have survived without his family. They'd embraced him with a careful balance of unconditional and tough love. No more enabling or ignoring his drinking as they'd done in the past. At thirty-two, he was living with his mom and dad. Two to three weekends a month, he stayed with his older sister, Ava. His younger brother, Sam, lived in Seattle, but he visited when he could to give their parents a break. Josh was only alone if he chose to be, which wasn't often. He couldn't afford to fail.

Stay sober.

That was his entire focus.

"I'm fortunate." Josh never thought he'd say those words, let alone believe them, but he had people who loved him on the days he hated himself. "I didn't know when I moved to Berry Lake why I needed to be back home, but it was the right decision."

Jenny touched his forearm. "You'll get through this."

Or I'll die trying.

Her fingers on his skin comforted him. Josh

fought the urge to inch closer, trying to ignore how he longed to have a woman in his life. This wasn't the time. In rehab and therapy, he'd been told no dating for the first twelve months of his recovery. There might not ever be a time for that. Even before he'd lost himself to the inside of a bottle, he'd never been good at relationships due to being, as more than one woman had said, too selfish and arrogant.

"Thanks." He'd imagined such a different future for himself—a successful football career, a beautiful wife, and happy kids. He'd had the first until an injury two and a half years ago sidelined him forever.

Not being able to play the game he loved had filled him with bitterness. Sure, he'd been hired at a ridiculous salary to provide commentary on football games and earned rave reviews, but that hadn't been enough to fill the void of not suiting up each week. Nor had it helped the pain in his leg that was a constant reminder of what he'd lost due to an illegal hit. His only relief had come while drinking, and it hadn't taken long before he couldn't get by without alcohol.

He swallowed around the shot glass-sized knot in his throat. "I have no choice if I want to keep my job."

Not that he needed to work. Thankfully, he hadn't blown through his money due to smart investments by his financial advisor, but his broadcasting career was all he had left of football.

His reputation was in ruins due to the arrest. Women selling their stories about his drunken nights with them to tabloids hadn't helped, either. His job was the only way to salvage a career that had him gracing the cover of sports magazines and being a hero to young players.

Her expression tightened. "That's... serious."

"They could have fired me, but an executive at the network went through something similar, so he's had my back."

For how much longer remained to be seen with exhibition games starting in August.

"Is there anything I can do to help?" Jenny asked earnestly.

Her words touched him because he deserved nothing from her. "You're doing it by talking to me now, but I'd like to do something for you."

This was the real reason he'd visited her. An apology was only words. He needed to show Jenny he'd changed. That he wasn't the same man he'd been the last time they'd been together.

"I can't undo our date, but—"

"You apologized. That's enough." Jenny spoke fast. "I forgive you, Josh. Nothing else is necessary."

Her words soothed his soul. "Thanks, but making amends is part of my recovery. Whether you need someone to watch your house when you get married, fly you to a book signing, or whatever else you might think of, I'm at your service. My plane, too."

Her eyes clouded. "Josh..."

"You don't have to decide right now." Even

though he wished she would. "My family will be honest with you about my flaws, and my flying abilities if you want to ask them."

As her gaze narrowed, she studied him without any judgment. "Doing something for me is important to you?"

He nodded, trying not to show how much he needed to do... this.

Jenny bit her lip. "I was planning to ship items for the wedding, but would you be willing to fly them to South Carolina for me in June?"

Josh straightened. "Yes. Tell me when. I'm on a leave of absence from work. My schedule is completely flexible."

"The wedding is on the second Friday in June. A few days before would be ideal." She smiled. "I need my dress there ahead of time to have it steamed."

"Happy to help." Relief brought a smile to his face. "Where in South Carolina?"

"Indigo Bay. It's a small beach town."

He'd never heard of the place. "Is that where your fiancé is from?"

"No, Dare's from New Hampshire but stationed in Georgia. We thought the East Coast was the best place to get married since it's only Missy and me here." As Jenny spoke to Josh like he was a friend, warmth flowed through him. "Dare's staff sergeant recommended Indigo Bay after spending Christmas there with his wife."

"I'll fly whatever you need there. Whenever." His gaze locked on Jenny. He hoped his gratitude shone through. "This will take a leap of faith on your part, but I won't let you down. I promise."

She squeezed his arm. "I trust you, Josh."

"Thanks." He only wished he trusted himself.

2

Natural light flooded Hope Ryan's studio, aka the converted guest bedroom in her twin brother's beach house. The sunshine was typical for late May in Indigo Bay, but special UV coating on the studio's windows and French doors kept the sunrays from damaging her art.

Art.

Yeah, right.

Stifling a yawn, Hope picked up the ornament to examine the miniature seascape. This was number twenty-seven of the thirty she was making to go into tin wedding favor buckets she'd decorated.

She tilted the wood piece to the right. Looked good. She angled the heart-shaped ornament to the left. The way the light hit made the Atlantic Ocean too blue and the grass on the beach too yellow. Her shoulders sagged.

With a sigh, she tossed the piece into the garbage can. The wood clattered against the metal. She grabbed another whitewashed wooden heart, and then sketched the shoreline onto the front.

After doing so many this week, the drawing took shape quickly, but she was dragging. Her heavy eyelids kept wanting to close. Hope knew the reason—not enough sleep.

Last night, she'd worked late at an anniversary party, but woken at her usual time this morning. Balancing her art with her new part-time job working events at the Indigo Bay Cottages Resort wasn't as easy as she thought it would be.

The door to the studio opened. Less than five seconds later, the scents of burgers and fries filled the room. Her stomach grumbled.

She smiled at her twin. Von's sandy-blond hair, the same color as hers, fell to his shoulders in loose waves. He wore jeans and a T-shirt. Both were clean, which suggested he hadn't been working on the houses he flipped for a living. Lately, he'd been spending more time in Charleston. She missed having him around.

Hope eyed the two bags he carried. "Please tell me there's a cheeseburger for me."

He grinned, a twinkle in his eyes. "I got you two."

"Exactly what I need." Von wasn't only her brother, but also her roommate and white knight.

"There's seasoned fries, too." Heavy footsteps—the steel-toed work boots he wore on jobsites—sounded against the tile floor he'd installed to make cleanup easier. "Figured you skipped breakfast and lunch."

"I did." Hope set the ornament on the workbench Von had made her. She didn't need to worry about much thanks to her brother. "I'm trying to get a project finished this week."

"What are you making?" he asked.

She hadn't told him about her latest commission yet. "Wedding favors."

As his jaw jutted forward, his shoulders and neck tensed.

Uh-oh. She knew what was coming, and tried to prepare herself.

His green eyes resembled the sea during a storm: dark and murky. "You should paint on a canvas instead of a small heart."

This was why she hadn't told him. She hated disappointing Von, but that was all she seemed to do with her art. Or what was left of it.

She raised her chin. "This is what I do now."

"That's because you gave up."

Hope flinched at his unexpected and hurtful words, but her brother had never been one to hold back. He'd told her not to marry Adam Darby too soon, but she hadn't listened. Oh, how she wished she had, then maybe she wouldn't have had to leave her dreams behind in New York. "You, of all people, know I had no choice."

Her muse, creativity, whatever one called the spark that ignited her passion, had deserted her—as had the players in the art world who'd once sung her praise. Sides had been picked, and she'd come out the loser over her ex-husband, whose lies had been believed over the truth.

"I don't know why you're bringing this up now," she added.

"Because you're wasting your talent. You should be creating art that's on display in galleries. Not stuck to the front of refrigerators or hanging on Christmas tree branches."

He'd said the words before, but they were never easy to hear. Von meant well. He supported her as no one else had, but she wished he'd let go of her old career and what she used to paint.

She had.

"I make decent money off the magnets and ornaments," she explained for what felt like the hundredth time. "Few artists living in a small town like Indigo Bay can say that."

Granted, she didn't pay much to live in his house. Well, one of them. Her brother also owned a townhome near Charleston where he stayed when he had a project there, several vacation rentals along the coast, and whatever investment properties he was working on. With real estate and contractor's licenses, he'd opened his own property investment company. At twenty-eight, his long hours and hard work were starting to pay off.

Von reached into the garbage can, pulled out the heart ornament, and shook his head. "You're better than this, Hope."

Once upon a time, she had been.

Now, not so much.

She understood her brother's mix of concern and disappointment, but... "I like what I do."

"You used to love it."

True. Too bad she wasn't strong enough to try again. She doubted she ever would be after failing in her previous attempts.

At Christmastime, she'd spent a day at the local gallery on Main Street, painting ornaments and personalizing them for customers. Doing that had been a huge, anxiety-ridden step for her. She hadn't wanted to book another time slot even though the gallery wanted her back.

"I am working on something new. Look what Zoe hired me to make." Hope motioned to the far wall. "I have a couple more to go, but I think they're looking good."

Von inhaled sharply before approaching the vertical fabric panels hung up to dry. Each contained a large seascape done using acrylic paint, not the oils she used to prefer. She had painted nothing near this scale in two years. Two long years of thinking she'd never create substantial work again. Not that these were art, per se, but…

"These are incredible, sis." Awe filled Von's voice. The tension seeped from his shoulders. He reached out, but then pulled his arm to his side as if remembering the panels were wet. "What are they for?"

"A wedding reception at the resort in June." She thought he'd like the romantic, beach-inspired panels. "They'll hang on the walls in the multi-purpose room. Tulle, seashells, and white fairy lights will go around them."

"Impressive."

Not compared to what she'd painted in the past, but working on the panels fed her soul in a way nothing else had since she'd left New York in disgrace. Hope had dreamed of being an artist with shows in popular galleries and write-ups in the paper. She'd succeeded for a few years until returning to Indigo Bay a total failure—her reputation ruined, her heart broken, and her trust in anyone but her family gone.

"If Zoe likes the panels, I'm hoping she'll hire me to paint seasonal ones."

"She'd be crazy not to love these."

"You're my brother. You have to like them."

Still, a smile tugged at Hope's lips. Von had found her the job with Zoe Ward, who worked in guest services and did event planning for the resort because he thought Hope needed to get out of the house more.

When he worked in Charleston, days went by without her seeing another person unless her friend and next-door neighbor, Paula O'Neill, dropped by. Not only was Hope around more people now, but she'd also been hired to make favors and decorations for events. A win-win.

"Others will, too." Von glanced over his shoulder at her. His smile lit up his face. "You should do more things like this."

Hope wanted to, but she shrugged. "I might if the gallery thinks they'll sell."

"Go there this afternoon. Show them photos of these. See what they say."

He hated her tourist tchotchkes, as he called them, but she didn't know why he was pushing her lately. Okay, it had been two years since she returned to Indigo Bay. Maybe that was the reason.

"First…" he continued. "You need to eat before you pass out from lack of food."

"I'm not starving," she teased.

"I hear your stomach growling from here." Von shot her a how-hard-is-it-to-remember-to-eat look. "Go wash up."

Von was two minutes and forty-two seconds older. He was her brother and her best friend. It was just the two of them in Indigo Bay since their parents had moved to Arizona. Mom and Dad spent their summers living in their RV and being hosts at a national park somewhere. A good retirement for them, but they never had time to visit, not even in the wintertime. Hope didn't know what she'd have done if Von hadn't taken her in.

Hope washed her hands before joining him in the kitchen. Their lunches were on plates at the breakfast bar with napkins and large glasses of sweet tea she'd made yesterday beside them.

"Thanks." Hope hopped onto a stool, shoving a French fry into her mouth at the same time.

"You need to eat more." He'd eaten half his burger already. Guess he was hungry, too.

"I eat." She grabbed two more fries.

"Not when you get wrapped up in a project." The concern in his voice was typical Von.

"You're the same way." She bit into the cheeseburger. So tasty.

"I remember to feed myself." He sipped his tea. "I'm not always going to be around to make sure you're taking care of yourself."

"That sounds ominous," she joked.

Von didn't look at her. Instead, he sighed.

Wait a minute. Her brother didn't sigh. "What's going on?"

His lips parted, but then he pressed them together.

Her chest tightened. "Von…"

"I met someone on a project last month. Her name's Marley. She's an architect. Smart. Beautiful. Everything I didn't know I needed in my life." The words flew from his mouth in a rush, one on top of the other. "I'm falling for her. Hard. I think I love her."

"Wow." Hope stared at her brother. A part of her knew this would happen someday, but another had hoped it would be later rather than sooner. "You mentioned going out with someone in Charleston, but I had no idea things were moving so fast."

He half-laughed. "Neither did I, but Marley makes me so… so happy. Are you okay with me having a girlfriend? A serious one?"

Hope hated the guilt in his voice. "Okay that the person I love most in the world is happy and in love? I'm thrilled."

Yes, she was surprised. To be honest, she might need time to come to terms with how this would change things between her and Von, but other than that…

"You deserve this." Her brother did. Von hadn't had much luck with relationships in the past due to picking the wrong women. Just as she'd picked the wrong men.

A twin thing?

She hoped Marley would be not only good *for* Von, but also good *to* him. "I guess this is why you've been spending more time in Charleston."

A sheepish smile crossed his face. "I have two projects going on there, but yeah. Marley is a Charleston native. Her entire family lives nearby."

Hope's breath hitched. She fought a rising panic. "Are you moving there?"

"No." He rubbed his lips together. "Maybe eventually, if things go further…"

"It's okay." The words rushed out. She didn't want Von to think she didn't support him one hundred percent.

His relieved gaze met hers. "Really?"

"I don't expect you to remain single and keep me company until we're old and gray."

Hope kept her voice lighthearted. She might have imagined that scenario once or twice, but that would never be enough for Von, even if she never wanted to date again. Forget marriage. Once was enough.

He hugged her. "You'll always have a place here. No matter where I end up living."

"Thanks." She soaked up her brother's warmth and strength before letting go of him. "When do I get to meet Marley?"

"Soon." His gaze softened, suggesting he was thinking about his girlfriend. "I hated keeping this from you, but I wanted to make sure there was something real between Marley and me."

"You didn't have to do that." Hope's family saw her as a fragile artist, inflexible and easily broken. Maybe she'd been that way when she'd returned from New York, but no one would break her again. "I'm not jealous of those with successful relationships. Especially you."

"After Adam…"

She didn't want to talk about her ex-husband. "I'm

happy for you and Marley. There's no need to go into overprotective-brother mode and worry about my feelings."

Von tapped his finger against the tip of her nose. "Overprotective *older* brother."

That made her laugh. "But please promise you'll listen to your friends or me if there are concerns or doubts about your new girlfriend."

Hope hadn't done that with Adam. She'd ignored the warnings, wanting to listen to her heart instead of the people who knew her best.

"Now who's being overprotective?" Von nudged her with his shoulder. "Don't worry. Your jerk of an ex taught us both hard lessons. I'm not about to forget them."

"Neither will I."

Hope couldn't. Her love for Adam Darby had given him the power to destroy everything that mattered to her. She wouldn't let that happen. Not ever again.

3

On the second Tuesday in June, Josh parked his rental car next to the Indigo Bay Cottages guest services building. Sitting behind the steering wheel, he replied to texts from his family and his sponsor, who'd called after he arrived in Charleston and wanted to know when he reached Indigo Bay.

His family could track him with their cell phones, but they preferred him checking in via text or phone. Given all they'd done and were doing for him, he didn't mind too much. This time was all about accountability to them and himself.

After he'd finished replying to everyone, Josh slid out of the rental car. He'd stopped for fuel and food along the way, but getting into a car after flying cross country made his bad leg ache more than normal. Taking a minute to stretch, he hoped to loosen up the tightness and work out the kinks. Better.

Waves crashed to shore to his left, but no pleasant sea breeze blew off the Atlantic. The humidity and heat made his clothes stick to him. All he wanted was a shower. First, though, he needed to check in and drop off the thank-you presents from Jenny. After he did that, he would have nothing left to do during his stay except play tourist, attend the wedding, and keep out of trouble—aka staying sober.

With two gift bags in hand, he made his way inside. The cool air refreshed him.

"Welcome to the Indigo Bay Cottages." A woman in her late thirties or early forties greeted him from her desk situated between two pillars and potted plants. As she stood, she smiled politely. She had dark hair and brown eyes and wore light blue shorts and a floral-print blouse. The ensemble was more business casual than beach attire. "I'm Zoe Ward. May I help you?"

Recognizing the woman's name, he appreciated her warm welcome. One of the gift bags he carried was for her. "I'm here for the Hanford-O'Rourke wedding. I have a reservation. Josh Cooper. Though it may be under my brother's name, Sam."

Zoe typed at her computer before grabbing a folder and a set of keys. "It's under both your names. Jenny told me you'd be arriving today with her gown."

Josh nodded, impressed Zoe remembered the wedding details. "I dropped it off at the dry cleaner on my way over."

The less time the gown was in his possession, the less chance he'd have of screwing it up and disappointing Jenny.

"Great," Zoe said brightly. "The bride won't have to worry about that when she arrives, then."

Speaking of the bride…

"This is for you from Jenny." Josh handed Zoe the gift bag with her name on it. The weight and shape told him a hardcover book was likely inside, but pink tissue paper kept the contents hidden. "She appreciates the planning you've done for her and Dare's wedding."

Zoe's eyes widened. "We aim to please at Indigo Bay, but Jenny didn't have—"

"She wanted to," he interrupted, not understanding why people couldn't simply accept a gift or a favor. Few seemed to get that the person doing the giving was receiving something, too. That was how he'd felt making amends.

A pleased smile curved Zoe's lips. "That's so nice of her."

Nice didn't begin to describe Jenny Hanford and her endless amount of compassion. Since he'd apologized, she'd asked him to meet her one morning a week at the cupcake shop where Missy worked… much to the surprise, or perhaps delight, of the town gossips. Jenny was becoming his closest ally outside his family, and she'd gone a step farther by inviting him to the wedding.

"Jenny would have delivered this herself, but she

27

was afraid she might forget to pack it."

"Weddings do that to a person, no matter if it's a large gathering or a more intimate affair." Zoe's gaze traveled from the gift bag to Josh before handing him the folder and keys. "You're staying in the cherry-red cottage."

"My brother made the reservation. I wasn't sure what he booked." He reached for his wallet. "I'll give you a credit card."

She glanced at her computer screen. "It's been taken care of."

Leave it to his brother. Sam wouldn't mention this until he wanted something—say the last slice of their mother's homemade chocolate silk pie.

As the image of one of their loud family dinners formed in Josh's mind, he nearly laughed. Those meals were one of the better things about being back in Berry Lake. "Thanks."

"Would you like to know a little bit about Indigo Bay Cottages?" Zoe asked.

"That would be great."

"This is the guest services building. If you need anything during your stay, let us know by dropping in or using your room phone. We have maps and info about sightseeing in town and the general vicinity. We're happy to make dinner reservations or have food delivered."

This was his first and likely only vacation this year—one he'd never expected to be taking on his own. He wasn't sure what he wanted to do, but going out to a restaurant by himself wasn't on his list. Delivery would be the best option.

"Are there menus in the cottage?" he asked.

"You'll find a binder with the info you need in the kitchen." Zoe's smile never wavered. "Jenny and Dare's wedding ceremony will be on the beach out front on Friday afternoon. A dinner reception will follow in the multipurpose room across the courtyard."

"Convenient."

"Vacations should be," Zoe said in a matter-of-fact tone. "The cottage interiors are decorated to match the exterior paint color. Each has a sitting area and kitchen. The size depends on the floor plan. Yours is one of our most popular two-bedroom cottages with incredible views and a great location. You're a short walk to Main Street and all Indigo Bay has to offer."

"Sounds great." Except one bedroom wouldn't be used. Sam's vacation request to the police department where he worked had been denied. "I'm on my own, though. My brother couldn't make it."

"If you get lonely, Indigo Bay is full of friendly faces who are always happy to chat with visitors."

"Thanks."

He hoped his brother not being here was the only glitch in his plan to stay until Sunday. So what if this was the longest he'd been on his own since entering rehab?

Josh would make the most of this trip. He would

prove to his family and to himself that he could handle this time away. Otherwise, he would never get on with his life.

Almost eleven months of sobriety. An uneventful cross-country flight. A place where only die-hard football fans might know about his troubles.

Indigo Bay sounded like the perfect getaway. His sponsor had also given him a list of meeting times in the area in case he needed extra support. Rudy did all he could to support Josh and said to call whenever, whether things were going good or bad. What could go wrong?

"Do you have any questions for me?" Zoe asked in a pleasant customer-service tone.

Josh remembered the other gift bag. "Jenny sent something for the artist who made the wedding favors."

"That's Hope Ryan, my assistant. She's working in the multipurpose room if you want to give it to her now."

"I would."

Zoe pointed to her right. "Go out the side door and across the courtyard. You can't miss it."

"Thanks."

He headed outside, and then through a pair of double glass doors. Large vertical painted panels hung on the wall facing him. The landscapes with dunes, grass, and the ocean in the background made him feel as if he were standing on the sand, not inside on a hardwood floor. Incredible artwork.

To his left, a blonde stood near the top rung on a ladder. Jean shorts showed off long, lean legs. Her pink t-shirt inched up at the back, giving a glimpse of smooth, honey-colored skin. She stretched on her tiptoes to attach the top of a panel to a clip.

That looked sketchy.

The ladder shifted.

Josh ran toward her. "Be careful."

She swayed, arms sticking out as if trying to balance herself, but the ladder tipped over. The woman fell, limbs flailing.

He stepped forward to break her fall. Somehow, she landed in his arms. The breath he'd been holding rushed out.

"I've got you." He stayed upright without dropping the gift bag, folder, or keys. Then again, he'd spent over half his life making sure he held onto the football no matter who was about to tackle him.

Catching her was unexpected. Not unenjoyable. She didn't weigh much, was soft in the right places, and smelled like strawberries.

His pulse quickened. Something that hadn't happened with a woman in months. He wasn't in any hurry to let go of her. At least until she shifted positions, wiggling as if she wanted down.

Yeah, this was more awkward for her than him.

Josh placed her on her feet but kept his hands on her waist to make sure she was steady. She was tall.

Around five-nine to his six-three.

"Are you okay?" he asked.

Her cheeks a bright pink, she nodded.

She was thin, not the healthy kind. If his mom were here, she'd make the woman eat a meal and two desserts. "You sure?"

"Yes."

The woman, who he assumed to be the artist, raised her chin, letting him see her hazel-colored eyes—more green than brown with gold flecks. Her pretty face was makeup free, but her clear skin, high cheekbones, and full lower lip didn't need anything extra.

"Thanks for catching me," she said, almost breathless.

"Glad I was around." She was attractive in a girl-next-door kind of way. He'd always preferred women with perfect makeup and designer clothes... camera ready was the term he used. "The floor might have hurt."

Her gaze dropped to the hardwood before returning to his. "I hope I didn't hurt you."

"You didn't." Linemen hit harder. Josh was standing too close for strangers, so he stepped back. "Are you Hope, the one making Jenny's wedding favors?"

"I am. "Hope's cheeks turned redder. "Are you the groom? I mean, Dare?"

"No, I'm Josh Cooper, a friend of Jenny's from

her hometown." He felt comfortable calling himself a friend after the times they'd spent together over the past month. Holding up the gift bag, he said, "She wanted you to have this."

"That's so thoughtful." Hope sounded touched, a shy smile gracing her lips as she took the gift. "Jenny sounded so sweet when we spoke on the phone."

"She is."

As Hope peeked inside the bag, a lock of hair fell across her face. Josh fought the urge to push the strands behind her ear to see her face better.

What was going on? He wasn't interested in a vacation romance. Even if he were, he was in recovery. No dating for twelve months. He'd heard that during his stay in rehab, at the sober house, and in therapy.

His interest, if he wanted to call it that, had to be due to holding her so closely, intimately. He was male, and he was missing physical contact. Something he'd had plenty of before rehab. When he'd been drinking—okay, while he'd been playing football, too—there'd been a revolving door of women coming in and out of his life. For months, there'd been none.

"Thanks for delivering this."

Hope's words jolted him back to reality. "Did you paint the panels?"

"Yes."

Her satisfied smile zinged through him like a pinball, bouncing off parts and lighting up his insides. Not pretty—*beautiful*. He gulped.

His reaction was unexpected and unwelcome. Maybe he should call Rudy or Dr. Kettering to see what they had to say about his attraction to Hope. Granted, looking was different than touching. On purpose touching. Catching her didn't count, but Josh didn't want to make any mistakes. Not when he'd come so far.

Hope studied the opposite wall where more panels hung. "My boss, Zoe, wants the room to look less multipurpose-ish for social events, starting with this weekend's wedding."

"You succeeded." Thankful to have something else to look at other than Hope, he took in the various panels. Each fit together as if part of a panorama. "You've brought the outside in."

"That was the plan."

"It's perfect." Josh was far from an art expert, but he'd been to galleries and recognized talent, even if the panels weren't typical canvases or tapestries. "You're good at what you do."

She kept her gaze lowered. "Thanks."

He waited for her to say more—the creative types he'd met might be introverts, but once their art was mentioned they lit up and wanted to talk. Hope, however, didn't. That intrigued him. Was she shy or embarrassed about winding up in his arms?

"You're welcome," he said finally.

She wiped her palms over her shorts. "I better get back to work."

No way was she hanging that panel by herself. If he hadn't caught her, she could have broken a bone or hit her head. He didn't mind putting off his shower.

Josh picked up the ladder. "Want help?"

* * *

Help? Hope's heart beat triple-time. No doubt from the shock of falling and being caught by a stranger.

A tall, handsome stranger with thick brown hair named Josh. His chiseled cheekbones, straight nose, full lips, and stunning blue eyes fit together as if created by a master painter. He had a body that would cause a sculptor to drool.

Her, too.

He must work out. Physiques like his didn't just happen. His navy polo shirt stretched across his wide shoulders, chest, and muscular arms. Not bulky body-builder muscles. His were leaner. Faded, well-worn jeans showed off his trim waist, flat abs, and clung to his thighs.

Stop staring at him.

Hope had been burned by one gorgeous guy who'd vowed to love and cherish her forever. Getting distracted by another man with a pretty face and killer body was stupid. The artist in her must be captivated by the aesthetic beauty of him. Nothing more.

She raised her gaze to his face.

Amusement glinted in his blue eyes.

Busted. Hope bit her cheek. He'd caught her checking him out, but he had no idea she wasn't interested in him *that* way. She'd rather go on a liquid diet of green and orange vegetables than date again.

Josh held onto the ladder. "I'll help you."

The last thing Hope wanted was *his* help. She wanted to hear him say goodbye before he walked out the door. If he was here for the wedding, however, he was likely staying at the cottages. Dallas, the resort's owner, and Zoe, her boss, took customer service seriously. Hope needed to be polite and not offend Josh. Otherwise, she might get in trouble or worse... lose her job.

"Thanks for the offer, but you should spend your time exploring this beautiful town." She kept her tone steady, her breathing even, and her gaze on the panel hanging haphazardly by one large clip. "I hung the other panels, and I only have two left to do."

"You did a fine job."

His rich voice washed over her like melted butter. Awareness thrummed through her. She opened her mouth to speak, but the words remained lodged in her dry throat.

What was happening to her? The last time she'd felt this way was when she met Adam at an exhibit. The heady rush had led to a living nightmare that still haunted her.

Never again.

She would remind herself that until the words sank

Melissa McClone

in.

Her heart had no other purpose than keeping her blood pumping. Loving another man, even liking or being attracted to one, wasn't allowed. Okay, maybe that was a bit extreme, but she'd removed herself from the dating scene—permanently.

Time to say goodbye to Mr. Josh Cooper. A smile would soften her words. "Again, thank you, but I'm sure you—"

"I don't feel right leaving you to do this on your own." His concern didn't bother her, but the male interest in his gaze made her uneasy. "If you fall again—"

"I'll be more careful." He'd interrupted her, so she didn't mind doing that to him. "I'm sure you have something better to do."

"Not really." A charming grin lit up his face, turning her insides to goo. "I arrived in Indigo Bay only a few minutes ago."

"Welcome to town." She tried to sound cheery. Maybe she could distract him, get him to leave. "I hope you enjoy your stay."

"It seems like a fun place to visit."

"If you like the beach and small towns, it is."

"I do." His gaze traveled from the top of her head to her canvas slip-ons. "Do you?"

Hope got the feeling he was teasing. Or flirting. That annoyed her. "Of course. I grew up here."

"And you're still here?"

She'd never planned to stay in Indigo Bay forever. Her goals had been too big for the small coastal town. Now that she was back, she often felt stuck, but this was home, and she was determined to make the best of her situation. Besides, where else would she go? But Josh didn't need to know all that.

Say as little as possible. "Lifer after a few years away."

That made him laugh. "I have an idea. I'll hold the ladder steady while you climb."

He wasn't letting this go. She blew out a breath. "I'm fine on my own."

"The other option is I ask Zoe to help you on my way out." His casual tone belied his serious gaze. "Which will it be?"

Neither option appealed to Hope. She didn't want to disturb her boss, nor did she want to fall again. If she got hurt, Hope would be in trouble. Especially with a long drive to Nashville tomorrow. Though being around Josh any longer might open herself up to a different kind of trouble.

She wet her dry lips. If she did this quick… "Hold the ladder, and I'll climb."

He repositioned the ladder near the wall. "Ready when you are."

She wasn't ready for this…

For him.

But the panels had to be hung before she left town in the morning.

With a breath to steady her nerves, she climbed the ladder. One rung, two, three.

"You don't need to go all the way to the top," he cautioned.

His concern was clear, but so was his arrogant stance and swagger when he moved. Once she finished with the panels, she would avoid the man.

"I've done this before." She didn't need someone else telling her what to do. Von was enough. Speaking of which, her brother wouldn't be happy if he found out she'd climbed with no one else around. A good thing he'd never find out.

As she went up the rungs, the ladder didn't sway as it did the last time. Must be Josh. His arms and legs looked strong. Not many guys could catch someone without stumbling or falling themselves.

Stop thinking about him.

She hooked the second clip to the fabric panel she'd been hanging when she fell. The tulle, lights, and garland would hide the hardware holding everything in place, but the florist was handling that part.

"Finished." Hope climbed off the ladder. Pointing to the space where the next one would go, she said, "I'll get the final panel in place now."

The piece lay on the floor. She'd had to roll the panels to transport them in her car. She was hanging them today to make sure they'd lay flat against the wall by Friday.

Josh repositioned the ladder before grabbing the

end of the panel. "You don't need to drag it yourself when there are two of us here."

His eagerness to help should have surprised her, but didn't, given him holding the ladder and dropping off the gift bag. Still, she had to ask, "Were you a Boy Scout when you were younger?"

He grinned. "No, I was too into sports, but my brother made it all the way to Eagle Scout."

"Mine, too." Josh being an athlete made sense given how fit he appeared. Together, they carried the panel to the ladder. "Ready?"

"Wait."

As if transporting a precious piece of art, he gently placed his end of the panel on the ground and straightened the piece to remove the creases.

His care touched her heart. Well, her artist heart. Few understood what the acrylic-painted panels meant to her. This attractive stranger didn't, but he'd still treated the pieces with respect. That eased some of her frustration with him but didn't change the fact she wanted him out of here ASAP.

He returned to the ladder, holding it steady by gripping the sides. "Now, you're good to climb."

"Thanks." She wanted to be upset with him for forcing her to accept his help, but his actions made her feel cared for. A way only Von and Paula had made her feel. They'd watched out for Hope since she'd been back in Indigo Bay. Feeling this way was disconcerting given she knew nothing about Josh except his name and that he was a friend of the bride.

"You okay?" he asked.

Oh, no. How long had she been lost in her thoughts?

"Fine." She arranged the panel in front of the ladder, maneuvering to climb while lifting it.

"Stop." Josh sounded alarmed. "You're not holding onto the ladder."

"I have to hold the panel."

"I'll pass it up to you when you get toward the top."

She hadn't thought of that, but she was used to doing things on her own. "Sounds safer."

His smile widened. "Much safer."

As she continued up, she didn't look at Josh. What if he was checking her out? What if he wasn't?

Pathetic.

One good-looking guy crosses her path, and she loses it? Maybe Paula was right when she'd said not dating would end up being Hope's downfall. Except she didn't want to date. She wanted nothing to do with men.

She stood near the top of the ladder. "I'm ready for the panel."

As he handed the piece up to her, Josh kept one hand on the ladder. "Here you go."

His gaze met hers. A woman could lose herself in those blue eyes. Any woman except her.

"T-thanks." The word sounded husky. Clearing

her throat, she clipped the panel into place and then climbed down. "I appreciate your help."

"You're welcome." He glanced around the room. "Be sure someone helps you take them down."

"I will." She shouldn't be disappointed he hadn't offered. Of course not. That would be ridiculous. He was a guest at the wedding, not hired help. "Enjoy your stay."

"First time here." He rubbed his chin. "Any places you recommend?"

"Sweet Caroline's Cafe has the best coffee and pie east of the Mississippi. It's on Main Street. Katie's Kitchen on Bayview is a great place for dinner. You can't go wrong with any restaurant in town."

"Thanks." His hand slipped around to the back of his neck. "Maybe I'll see you around."

"You will." The words slipped out before she realized what she was saying.

A smile brightened his face.

Her breath caught in her throat. She coughed.

"When?" he asked.

"Jenny and Dare's wedding," Hope clarified. "I'm working at it."

He puffed out a breath. "I'll see you then."

Funny, but he sounded disappointed. He turned and strode toward the door with a slight limp. Something she hadn't noticed before.

He glanced over his shoulder, lips quirking when he caught her staring.

Heat pooled in her cheeks. Her tongue felt ten sizes too big for her mouth, but something compelled her to talk to him. "Don't forget to wear sunscreen while you're out."

He raised a brow. "Sunscreen?"

Ugh. That was not what she'd planned on saying, but sunscreen was safer than asking if he wanted to meet her for coffee later. She was planning to stop by Caroline's before heading home.

Time for damage control. "I have a twin brother, and he never wears it. Sorry. Overprotective sister."

A beat passed. And another. "I have one of those, too. But she means well."

"So do I." Why couldn't Hope keep her mouth shut?

"I'll remember the sunscreen." Josh sounded amused. "See ya."

"Can't wait." *Oh, no.* Hope cringed. "I mean, for the wedding."

With a wave, he left the multi-purpose room.

She groaned. What in the world was wrong with her?

4

As Josh parked in front of the "cherry-red" cottage, he kept thinking about Hope Ryan. Catching and holding her wasn't against the rules since he'd saved her from injuring herself. The best part, however, had been talking to her. Oh, she hadn't trusted his offer to help, but he'd seen no pity or hatred in her eyes. That meant she hadn't recognized him.

That was good. So was the way she blushed.

Thinking about her pink cheeks brought a smile to his lips.

The fact she was on his mind wasn't an issue. He could recite the list of what he *couldn't* do in his sleep. Some things weren't exactly rules, but rather strong suggestions of what to avoid.

He had.

And would keep avoiding them.

But meeting someone new had been… nice. Speaking to women was fine. If he saw Hope again in town, he would approach her.

People in Berry Lake kept their distance from him except for his family, and, this past month, Jenny, but he was getting used to it. Other than his stint at the luxury rehab facility, the sober house, and a long weekend in a rented cabin on Mount Hood with Sam, Josh had stayed in town. That enabled him to remain under his family's watchful and loving eyes. A complete difference from when he'd lived alone, traveled each week to a new city to broadcast a game, and hung out with sexy women he'd met in hotel bars.

Regrets and longings swirled in his head.

He missed football. He missed female company. He missed… a lot of things.

Stop thinking about what's missing. Focus on what you have.

Josh inhaled, letting the sea air fill his lungs, and then stared at the cottage that would be his home until Sunday.

The white railing and Adirondack chairs stood out against the cherry-red color of the quaint structure. He climbed the steps, unlocked the front door, and stepped inside.

The faint scent of citrus filled the air. Wood-paned windows filled the comfortable space with sunlight. Not bad for a beach cottage.

An overstuffed red plaid couch, a red and white

striped chair, and a white wood coffee table formed a small living area next to a dining table with four red chairs. Red accessories gave the small kitchen with its white cabinets and counter a splash of color. The two bedrooms, each with their own bathrooms, were similar sizes, so he took the closest one.

After a quick shower, he put on shorts, a T-shirt, and flip-flops. Time to check out the town.

With a baseball cap and sunglasses on, Josh headed to Main Street. Shops and restaurants lined each side. The sidewalks weren't too crowded. Couples strolled hand in hand. Kids ran to windows pointing and laughing. Memories of spending a week each summer on the Oregon coast with his family surfaced. The biggest difference between here and there, other than the passage of time, was the weather. He'd only been outside for fifteen minutes, but he was ready to cool down.

A sign for Sweet Caroline's Cafe was ahead. Hope had recommended the place for coffee and pie. He didn't need either of those things—he'd become a tea drinker during rehab—but something cold to drink would hit the spot. Sitting for a few minutes wouldn't hurt, either. His leg wasn't bothering him for once, but he was tired after the long flight.

Ducking inside the shop, he removed his sunglasses. The cool temperature brought instant relief. The delicious scents of baked goods made his mouth water. He'd have to come back when he was in the mood for dessert.

An older couple stood in line ahead of him. He stared at the menu board behind the counter.

The din of conversations from customers reminded him of the shops and restaurants in Berry Lake. He hadn't been to those places by himself since a customer at the bagel shop cursed at him. Under-the-breath comments he could handle, but the to-his-face remarks had made him crave a drink, so he'd stopped going out alone.

Maybe someday, he'd feel comfortable on his own in his hometown. Or maybe Berry Lake wasn't the place for him long-term. Only time would tell.

As the couple in front of him headed to the seating area, an attractive fifty-something woman with shorter brown hair motioned him toward the counter.

"Welcome." The warmth in her eyes matched her smile. "I'm Caroline, and this is my cafe."

"Nice place," he said, liking the inviting atmosphere. "I'd like to order a drink."

"Are you in the mood for something hot or cold today?"

"Cold." He glanced at the menu board again. "How is the frozen hot chocolate?"

"Perfect for a warm day like today," she replied without missing a beat.

"I'll take one of those please."

As Caroline relayed what he wanted to a young apron-wearing barista, she rang up his order and took his twenty-dollar bill. "Have we met before?

Once upon a time, Josh thrived upon being recognized. Posing for selfies and signing autographs had made him and his ego happy. Now he hated people knowing who he was.

"Well, I arrived in Indigo Bay less than an hour ago." He tried to keep his voice steady when his insides twisted. "It's my first time here."

"I know you from somewhere." She tilted her head as if trying to figure out where. Her mouth opened. "You're Josh Cooper."

He nodded, fighting the urge to run back to the cottage.

Was it too late to ask for a to-go cup?

Yeah, he was a coward. A big old chicken.

For good reason.

Now when people recognized him, he never knew what they would focus on—his successful college years, his glory days as a pro-quarterback, his career-ending injury, his drinking and womanizing, or his arrest. Only two of the five were things he wanted to discuss, but even that could be uncomfortable.

He shifted his weight between his feet.

"I missed hearing you announce games last season." Her voice was low as if she wanted no one else to hear. "I always learned something new about football listening to you."

"Thanks." That was an unexpected compliment, but nice to hear. He viewed the field as a player, which made saying what was happening or what he thought would happen second nature to him. "I missed calling games."

Understanding filled Caroline's eyes. His troubles had been splashed over papers and on sports networks. If she recognized him, she likely knew what he'd been doing instead of broadcasting games. "Will you be in the booth this year?"

"That's the plan." He hoped it worked.

Caroline handed Josh his change. "Then you should make the most of your time here."

"I hope to." Sam not being with him could be a blessing in disguise. The time in Indigo Bay would show Josh if he could handle being on his own before the new season kicked off. Though his family would keep an eye on him, even from across the country.

"Where are you staying?" Caroline asked.

He tucked a dollar into the tip jar. "The Indigo Bay Cottages."

Caroline stood taller. "My son Dallas owns the resort. I'm the resident expert on Indigo Bay. If you'd like, I'm happy to help you and whoever you're traveling with figure out a sightseeing itinerary."

"Thanks. I'm on my own this trip, and I may take you up on that tomorrow." Josh appreciated how everyone in town had been friendly so far. "I should have flown over Indigo Bay before I landed in Charleston because I'm already tired from trying to get a feel for the town."

"You're a pilot."

It wasn't a question, but he nodded anyway. "I love flying."

"Where are you from?"

"Washington state."

"No wonder you're tired. This weather takes some getting used to if you're from the West." Caroline studied him. "Go sit. I'll bring out your drink when it's ready."

"Thanks." He faced the seating area. Most of the tables were full, but a few had empty chairs. Maybe he could snag one.

Josh took a step before noticing the back of a blonde wearing a pink T-shirt. That looked like Hope. He'd wanted to approach her if he saw her again. This was his chance.

With purposeful strides, he made his way to her table. A piece of berry pie, a glass of iced tea, and a cell phone laying screen down were in front of her.

He stood a foot away from her table. "Hope?"

Her eyes widened. "Josh."

"Hi." Something fluttered in his stomach. "I'm trying your first recommendation."

She shifted in her chair. "I hope you're not disappointed."

"I'll let you know."

That charming blush colored her cheeks. A smile tugged at her lips. "Oh, the pressure."

He grinned. "Given you're here, I'd say you're

safe."

Flirting was second nature. A sexy comeback was poised ready at the tip of his tongue, but this wasn't the time or place for that. He wasn't looking for a hookup. What he wanted was someone to talk to—a person who wasn't worried he'd stopped at a liquor store or carried a hidden flask.

Trust had to be earned.

Rudy kept stressing that.

Josh glanced around the seating area. "Most of the tables are taken. Mind if I sit with you?"

* * *

Hope managed not to frown, easy to do when Josh's words had frozen her expression and thoughts. *Say no.* Oh, she wanted to, but that would be rude. Not only to him, a guest at the resort where she worked, but also to the other tourists who might need a table for their parties. She was, in a word, stuck.

Story of her life.

Maybe one of these days, she could change that.

Hope motioned to the empty chair at her table. "Go ahead."

Somehow her voice remained steady, and her hand didn't shake, but her insides trembled.

As he sat, she tried not to stare.

If she'd thought Josh Cooper was attractive before, that was nothing to seeing him dressed in a pair of shorts and a plain navy T-shirt that made his eyes look bluer. Even his feet in flip-flops looked good.

Then there was his hair. Damp as if he'd swam or showered before coming here. She wanted to wrap one of the curly ends around her finger.

Trouble with a capital T.

Hope sipped her iced tea, but the drink didn't cool her down. If she ate more quickly, she could get out of here. She shoveled a forkful of the sweet mixed-berry pie into her mouth.

He leaned forward. "I live in a small town that's tourist oriented, but we only see big crowds when there's something special going on. Indigo Bay seems like the place to be this summer."

She focused on her pie, not his delicious scent—a mix of soap, water, and something distinctly male.

"The town is popular with vacationers. More people are visiting from out of state." She'd received a crash course about Indigo Bay tourism when Zoe hired her. "Some residents rent out their homes during the Fourth of July week due to the high demand for accommodations."

His gaze hadn't left Hope. "Where do they go?"

"Anywhere but here." The way he stared made her self-conscious. Maybe she had pie on her face. She wiped her mouth with a napkin. "It's a madhouse and crowded, but the influx of visitors with money to spend is great for local businesses."

"And your art?"

"My art is directed toward tourists. Holidays are good for me." She took another sip of her iced tea.

"Are your paintings on display in town?"

He was full of questions. She rubbed off a bead of condensation rolling down her glass. "The items I make are sold at the art gallery on Main Street and other shops in town."

"Have you shown your work outside Indigo Bay?"

"Not for a few years." She shoved a forkful of pie into her mouth. That gave her an excuse not to say more.

As if on cue, Caroline set a frozen hot chocolate in front of Josh. Hope had never been so happy to see Dallas' mom. Hope didn't like discussing her ex-husband or her art.

"Wow, this looks amazing." Josh brought the straw to his lips—full, soft lips that Hope had the urge to, um, sketch—and sucked. "Tastes even better."

Caroline's grin spread. "So happy you like it. How do the two of you know each other?"

"We met at the resort earlier." The less Hope said, the better. Indigo Bay was the kind of town where people liked knowing everyone's business, but after gossip spread two years ago following her divorce, she hated anyone talking about her—good or bad.

"Hope recommended your cafe to me," Josh added.

"Thank you, dear." Caroline's gaze traveled between Hope and Josh. Uh-oh. The cafe owner had the same look Lucille Sanderson got when she wanted to find a date for her great niece Maggie from Atlanta. "Josh is on his own. If you're available, maybe you could show him around tomorrow."

Not happening. Hope didn't need Caroline playing matchmaker. A good thing she wasn't free.

"I'm sorry, but I have plans." Her tone was sugary sweet, perfected after years of trying to convince her parents to send her to art camp each summer. "I'm driving to Nashville tomorrow."

Josh's mouth froze an inch above the straw before he straightened. "Aren't you working at Jenny and Dare's wedding on Friday?"

"I'll be back on Thursday." Hope ate another bite of pie.

"Wait a minute." Caroline's smile disappeared into a thin, tight line. "You're planning to drive over eight hours tomorrow, return the next day, and then spend Friday setting up for a wedding and working the event?"

Three days was nothing compared to the days she would paint without sleeping or eating. "Trust me. I'll be fine."

Caroline opened her mouth, shut it, and then tried again. "Is Von going with you?"

"Who's Von?" Josh asked.

"Her twin brother."

Hope didn't like being spoken about as if she weren't here. "Von has to work. I'm going by myself."

"No, no, no." Caroline shook her head. "That's too much driving. You'll be exhausted."

"I'm not going to fall apart if I'm a little tired." She'd survived a bad marriage and the destruction of her career. Two days of driving would be easy. Besides she had no choice. She couldn't say no to the couple who'd supported her. Tomorrow was the best day for them to hand off their damaged painting. "I'm spending tomorrow night in a motel."

Von had made the reservation when Hope wanted to drive there and back in one day. He still wasn't happy she was going, but he understood why she needed to do this.

"I don't mean to interfere, but Caroline's correct," Josh said. "You'll be more tired than you realize, especially working the wedding."

"Not only the wedding," Caroline added. "Zoe will expect you to setup and clean afterward."

"There's no need to tag team me. I know my schedule." Hope tried to keep her frustration out of her voice. She wasn't sure she succeeded. "And what I'm capable of doing."

Josh raised an eyebrow. "What if you're wrong?"

5

Forget thinking the man sitting across the table from her was attractive. Josh Cooper was nothing but annoying.

Hope raised her chin. "I'm not wrong. I won't be too tired to work on Friday."

His jaw jutted forward, making him look sexy and dangerous, like a bad boy from a romance novel come to life. A good thing she'd been married to an alpha male and was immune to them.

"I'm not trying to be a jerk or upset you, but I'd rather my friend's wedding not suffer if you're tired." Josh's tone wasn't icy, but the edge to his words told her this was important to him.

Fine, but he had no idea she used to paint for days with zero sleep and limited food. Her work might have slowed toward the end, but it never suffered. If anything, she tried harder when she found herself in the zone—the place where only the painting existed.

"Nothing will suffer." Despite feeling twisty and knotted inside, her words came out calm. She needed to act professional even if she wanted to dump the rest of her iced tea on his head. Yeah, that would be too much—too extra as Paula might say—and probably cost Hope her job, but something about Josh Cooper set her off even though they didn't know each other.

Strike that. She knew what it was. Adam had shown her that handsome and arrogant went together like salt and pepper. Attractive and nice was a harder combination to find.

Not that she was looking.

She stared down her nose at Josh. "I'm sure Jenny appreciates your concern, but I'll be able to do my job as required."

He tilted his head from one side to the other. "What if you have car trouble or can't get back to Indigo Bay in time for the wedding?"

"I've had no problems with my car." Von made sure of that. "But if I did, I'd call roadside assistance. I'm returning on Thursday. The wedding isn't until Friday afternoon. That gives me plenty of time if something doesn't go as planned."

"You have leeway, but it's not worth the risk." As the concern in Josh's eyes deepened, he rubbed his chin. "Jenny and Dare have been through so much to get where they are. Do you believe in fate?"

Hope had once thought something greater brought Adam into her life, but now… "No, I don't."

Josh's shoulders pushed back. "I do. It's a miracle Jenny and Dare found each other, even more of one that they fell in love once they did. They deserve to have a perfect wedding. I'll do what I can to make sure that happens."

The emotion in his voice surprised Hope. He must be a close friend of the bride to care this much.

Her annoyance faded. "What do you suggest?"

"Let me fly you to Nashville." He spoke as if he were offering her a ride to a mall in Charleston. "You'd be back in Indigo Bay tomorrow night—well-rested for the wedding on Friday."

Hope's mouth dropped.

Caroline clapped. Funny, but Hope had forgotten the woman was there. "That's a great idea, Josh. Flying will be quicker than driving. Safer, too. I'm sure Von would agree."

"I haven't agreed." Hope stared at Caroline, willing the cafe owner to back down. "I appreciate the offer, but a private plane will be too small for the painting I'm picking up."

"I have a lightweight jet." If Josh didn't look so earnest, Hope would think he was boasting. "Is the painting bigger than four by five?"

Who was this guy? Regular people didn't own planes or "lightweight jets." Although the bride was a bestselling author with movies being made from her books. Maybe she hung around other wealthy people. That was another strike against Josh. Hope kept her distance from rich people. That had been Adam's world.

"It's four by three," she answered.

A satisfied smile settled on Josh's face. "The painting will fit. Though you'll need to wrap it in case of turbulence."

"It's settled then." Caroline grinned like a kid who'd gotten what they wanted from Santa Claus. "I'll leave you two to discuss the details."

Hope sighed. "I haven't said yes."

"True." As Josh positioned the straw to his mouth, he winked. "But you haven't said no, either."

Unsure what to say, she finished her pie.

He appeared happy to drink his frozen hot chocolate in silence, but amusement lit his eyes.

The man was back to being annoying. Not that he'd stopped. "Is something funny?"

His mouth released the straw. "You are."

"Me?"

He nodded. "You aren't sure if you like me or not."

"I don't know enough about you to decide that." But she was leaning toward not liking him.

"If you fly with me to Nashville, we'll have plenty of time to get to know one another."

Nice segue. Not.

Hope wiped her mouth with her napkin, moving

slowly to give herself a moment before answering Josh's question. He was the definition of charming—she'd give him that—and, if she weren't careful, she might find herself on his plane without realizing how she'd gotten there. His concern and wanting to help Jenny reminded Hope of her brother.

"I'm still thinking about your offer," she said finally.

Part of her wanted to say no and be done with him, but the practical side didn't want to lose two days to driving. She prided herself on doing a good job, even if she were running on fumes, but she didn't want Josh mentioning the long drive to Zoe if something were to go wrong on the wedding day.

"When do you need an answer?" Hope asked.

"Later tonight." He sipped his frozen hot chocolate.

That sounded more than reasonable, more than how she couldn't seem to drag her gaze away from his lips on that straw. Best to be on her way before he caught her staring. Again.

"Sweet Caroline's is getting more crowded, and I'm finished with my pie." She pushed back her chair and stood. "I'll leave a message for you with guest services."

Rising as well, he pulled his cell phone from his pocket. "Exchanging numbers will be easier."

True, but only a handful of people had her number. That was on purpose. Still, she took his phone and texted herself. A beep sounded from her phone on the table. "You have mine now."

"Where are you going?" he asked, his eyes eager and a big grin on his face.

"Home. I need to finish a few ornaments." She pressed her lips together to keep from saying more. He didn't care what she needed to do tonight—like not freak out about whether she could find enough of her lost mojo to repair the damaged painting she would pick up tomorrow.

"I'll walk out with you."

She glanced to where his half-filled mug still sat on the table. "You didn't finish your drink."

"I've had enough." As they left the cafe, Josh held open the door for her. "Which direction are you going?"

"Toward the beach."

"Me, too."

Of course he was. She swallowed a sigh.

He fell into step next to her. "Indigo Bay is a quaint town."

"The place checks all the boxes for vacationers, but sometimes I wish…"

"What?"

"That there were fewer tourist-oriented places and more for full-time residents," she admitted. "Charleston isn't far. We have a hardware store and a few other places, so I shouldn't complain, but it's easy to feel stuck here."

"You need a vacation."

"Yes, I do." She hadn't been anywhere since she moved back from New York. "Though lots of people call this place a vacation spot."

"It's not the same when you live here full time." He stared into the window of Coastal Creations, Whitney Layton's jewelry store. "I'm from a small town called Berry Lake in Washington state. It has a Main Street similar to this one, but there's nothing nearby, so the town caters to both tourists and residents. A few times a year, people flock to festivals. By the last one, many residents are fed up, but several have that same stuck feeling due to their businesses or not wanting to leave their homes empty."

"That's what Fourth of July and Labor Day weekend are like here."

"I'm sure others living in similar places feel the same way." He slowed his pace to match hers. "I watched our sleepy little town turn into a tourist destination."

"Do you still live there?" she asked.

"I moved back last summer." He kept glancing at shop windows. "Before that, I lived in New York City."

Interesting they had that in common. "I lived in Manhattan for four years."

He raised a brow and opened his mouth, but then closed it.

"What?" she asked.

"Don't take this the wrong way, but you don't seem like the New York type."

She laughed because she was no longer that type. Never had been. "I had a closet full of black when I lived there."

Adam had hated the clothes she'd brought with her—saying they were too beachy or college-like. He'd made her throw those away and buy new outfits he'd picked out. All in one shade... black.

"Now I have a rainbow of colors to wear." Thinking of the clothes hanging in her closet brought a smile. "I prefer that."

Josh moved behind Hope to let a family of five pass. "New York seems like the perfect city for an artist. Why'd you come back to Indigo Bay?"

"A lot of reasons."

Ones she didn't want to go into details with Josh. She'd left this town full of promise before returning divorced and devastated. Only her brother and Paula knew the truth. Others had believed the lies and rumors.

There was one reason she didn't mind sharing. "Von went to college in Alabama, but he returned after graduation. It made sense for me to move back."

"Being near family is important."

She'd be lost without her brother. "Why'd you go back to Berry Lake?"

"Family," Josh said without hesitation. "My parents and older sister live there. My younger brother is a few hours away in Seattle. Sometimes a person needs a change but a familiar one."

She could relate to that. "I sure did."

Curiosity flared in his gaze, but he said nothing.

As she passed Mrs. Donovan's floral shop, the sweet fragrance of fresh-cut flowers in buckets lingered in the air. A watercolor of the storefront would be fun to paint. Well, not a painting, she corrected herself, but something else. She'd have to think about that more.

She made her way toward Seaside Boulevard where her and Josh would go their separate ways. Her brother's beach house was in the opposite direction of the Indigo Bay Cottages.

"Is there anything that might help you decide between flying and driving to Nashville?" Josh asked.

She thought the discussion about the flight was over. Guess not. "Not really," she admitted. "Truthfully, I don't step out of my comfort zone much. I need time to think about it."

"Are you afraid of flying?" he asked.

"No. I haven't flown that much, but flying doesn't bother me."

He brushed his hand through his hair. "Are you afraid to go with me?"

She stopped in front of the gift shop that sold her hand-painted Indigo Bay magnets and ornaments. "Not afraid, but I just met you. Caution seems prudent in this situation."

"Makes sense." His lips curved upward. Good, he didn't appear upset by what she'd said. "What's your gut instinct tell you?"

To stay away, but that was due to her issues, not Josh. "My instincts have been wrong in the past. That's why I take my time making decisions."

"If it helps, I'm a friendly guy."

She raised an eyebrow. "A few serial killers have been called friendly by those who knew them."

"You're going there, huh?" He chuckled. "I haven't killed anybody—though when my brother pushed me into the lake with my brand-new cell phone in my pocket, I thought about it."

She laughed. "A sympathetic jury might have let you off."

"Yeah, but my mom wouldn't have."

Joking around with Josh was fun, but she didn't understand those butterflies flapping around her stomach.

"Tell me about the painting you need to pick up," he said.

They were less than a block from where they'd go their separate ways. Hope needed to make this quick.

"I met Dan and Cami Mulholland five years ago at a gallery. They're art lovers. A fire recently destroyed their house. Only one of their paintings survived. They asked me to restore it if I can."

Hope left out the part that four of her other paintings had been burnt to ashes. The news had brought her to her knees, knowing those works were gone and she'd never add more to her portfolio.

"That's horrible." His brow furrowed. "Are they okay?"

Her stomach clenched when she remembered Cami's sad call a few days ago. "They got out without any injuries—their animals, too—but they lost so much. I don't know if I can repair their painting. The smoke and water damage are bad, but I need to try."

"I hope you can."

"Me, too." She blew out a breath, trying to stop the uncertainty over painting with oils again from overwhelming her. "They didn't want to ship the painting in case it got lost. I offered to go there to make it easier on them."

"You have a kind heart."

"Anyone would do it."

"But you're the one making the effort." He touched her arm, his fingertips rough against her skin. "I can't imagine what losing everything in a fire would be like. I want to help you bring the painting back to Indigo Bay."

The genuine tone of his voice wrapped around her heart like a hug. Saying no might be the smarter move, but he seemed sincere.

He dropped his hand to his side, and Hope missed his touch. Weird.

Maybe she was overanalyzing the situation. Josh was out of her league, even if he might have flirted with her a little earlier. Though she'd bet flirting came as natural as breathing to him. He might not even realize he was doing it. Von was like that.

"Please," Josh added, sounding more like a big kid than an adult.

That made her laugh. "If I say yes, I want to pay for your expenses."

"Not necessary. You're doing someone a favor."

"You will be, too, if you fly me there."

"I'd like to help out that couple, but I'm also doing this for Jenny and for me." He moistened his lips. "I've been trying to make up for some past mistakes. I'd love the chance to do this with you."

Josh's words made his offer that much sweeter. "Jenny's lucky to have a friend like you."

"I'd like to be your friend."

In a different place, under different circumstances, his words might be considered a pick-up line, but he wasn't putting a move on her. He only wanted to help. The question was—would she let him?

A beat passed. And another.

"You're not going to make this easy on me by just saying yes, are you?" He didn't sound upset, more surprised as if he were used to getting his way.

At the corner of Seaside Boulevard, she stopped. "I'm not trying to be difficult."

"You're not. You're being practical and safe, the way I'd want my sister to be if someone she didn't know offered to fly her somewhere."

"Thanks for understanding." Hope pointed to her left. "I live that way. I'll… be in touch."

"Don't go yet." There was a hint of urgency to his words. "You've spoken to Jenny on the phone. Why don't you talk to her again to get a character reference?"

He was more adorable than annoying right now. "I'm past thinking you're an axe murderer."

"Lucky me." He grinned. "But seriously, I understand why you want to take your time and contribute toward the flight."

"I hear a "but" coming."

"Not quite but close," he admitted sheepishly. "I was thinking of something you could do for me if I fly you to Nashville."

Hope straightened. "What?"

"Buy me lunch."

"Lunch?"

He nodded. "There's this barbeque joint I love. I eat there whenever I'm in Nashville."

"Paying for your meal isn't enough."

He rubbed his chin. "Money for fuel?"

She had no idea how much that would cost, but with her new job, she'd been putting part of her salary into savings each paycheck. "That would work."

"Then it's a go." His happy voice matched his smile. "I'll text you later to nail down where and when to meet in the morning."

"O-kay." Except she wasn't sure why he'd taken

her words "that would work" to mean "yes, she was going with him."

So why wasn't she correcting him instead of letting him walk away believing they'd made a deal?

6

The next morning, Josh rose with the sun. He'd slept better than he expected for his first night on his own, but anticipation for the flight to Nashville made him unable to sit still while he drank a cup of tea. A run would settle him.

As his feet pounded against the sand, he breathed in the sea air. Sweat dampened his hairline and dripped down his back. His muscles twitched. Nothing new given his leg had never truly healed after being snapped in two from a late hit. He ignored the pain. That would never go away, no matter how many surgeries he had or physical therapists he visited. He pushed through as he always did.

Only today was a little sweeter.

Not only would he be flying, but he'd also be spending time with Hope Ryan. She was...

challenging. Yeah, that seemed the right word. Women—at least before his arrest and rehab—flirted and wanted to spend time with him. Hope wasn't like that. She'd seemed ready to bolt both times he'd spoken to her yesterday. She hadn't accepted his offer to fly, but he'd taken a chance by acting as if she had because he wanted to help—Jenny, the couple who lost their house, and himself. Besides, he wouldn't mind getting to know Hope better, too.

If the phrase "wear her heart on her sleeve" needed a poster child, Hope would be it. Every feeling shone in her eyes and on her face. That included annoyance, attraction, frustration, and confusion.

Especially that last one.

One thing Hope hadn't been was impressed. That hadn't stopped her from checking him out, though, which his ego appreciated. He'd been fascinated by her—not in an I-want-to-date-her way, but more of an I-appreciate-her-talent-and-kindness way. He should swing by Sweet Caroline's to bring pastries and warm beverages for the drive to the airport in Charleston. Bet Hope would like that.

His phone rang.

He glanced at the screen—Sam.

Josh slowed his pace to take the call. "Back on third shift, bro?"

"For now." Sam sounded chipper for it being the middle of the night in Seattle. "I got your text. You're up early."

"I wanted to go for a run before taking off."

"Flying some chick to Nashville, huh?" Sam's casual words didn't mask his concern. "Is that a good idea?"

"Not some chick." Josh pictured Hope as he'd left her yesterday afternoon. Her befuddled expression had made him laugh all the way back to the cottage. But he'd gotten what he wanted, and she wouldn't have two days of driving ahead of her. No harm done. "Hope is an artist doing a favor for two friends. I'm helping her out."

"You've been helping a lot of people."

He settled into a brisk walking speed. "I have a lot to make up for."

"Is Hope someone you hurt with your drinking?"

"No." But that didn't mean he had to stop doing nice things. "We met yesterday."

"That means Hope must be a tall, leggy brunette."

"She's tall but blonde." Josh wasn't about to mention her long legs. "You know I'm not supposed to date for the first twelve months."

"Making sure you remember that."

"Hard to forget since any time I mention a woman's name, you guys mention that." Josh understood why they did, but his family made him feel like a kid who couldn't cross the street without someone holding his hand. "It's a flight to Nashville and back. If it were more, do you think I would have told you or Dr. Kettering about it?"

"You spoke to your therapist?"

"After I texted you." Josh hated explaining everything in his life to others, but he wanted to regain his family's trust. "Hope is pretty, but this isn't a man-woman thing. Even if that were in the realm of possibilities, it's Wednesday. I'm here until Sunday. Not a lot of time for anything to happen between then and now. If we get along, she'll be a new friend like Jenny."

"Okay, you do need more friends, even if they live on the other side of the country," Sam agreed. "I'm not trying to be an annoying younger brother. I'm watching out for you."

"I appreciate that, even if you are annoying."

"Haha."

The voice of a female dispatcher sounded in the background.

"Is that for you?" Josh asked.

"Nope." Sam snickered. "You're stuck with me for a few more minutes."

Josh was glad, but he wouldn't let Sam know, or he'd never live it down. "Lucky me."

"I'm the best brother ever."

Typical Sam. The kid didn't lack confidence. Never had. "You're my only brother."

"Still the best."

"And so modest," Josh teased.

"I learned humility from you."

Josh shook his head. "You might need homework

then."

"No way," Sam fired back. "I can be as big of a cocky SOB as you."

Josh had that reputation when he'd played football, though he'd backed it up on the field. He'd also been called arrogant by critics of his broadcasting abilities. Now… he had no idea who he would be if he returned to work.

When, not if, he corrected.

"What are your plans after you get back from Nashville?" Sam asked.

"Relaxing." Sitting in one of the chairs in front of the cottage sounded good. The crashing waves would make for a great soundtrack. He would have dinner delivered. Maybe eat outside if he could stand the heat and humidity. It wasn't too bad right now. "I'm also attending a meeting. After that, I'll read. I have two books to finish while I'm here."

Dr. Kettering loaned him a self-help book for the trip. He'd also brought Jenny's newest thriller.

"Wish I was there, bro." Sam's wistful tone surprised Josh. His brother was a go-with-the-flow kind of guy. "I need a vacation."

"We'll do something in July," Josh said. "Rent another cabin or go camping."

"Sounds good." Silence filled the line. "Keep me posted on your flights and when you're back in Indigo Bay."

Sometimes Sam acted more like the older brother

than the younger one. Josh would have to take back that role at some point but now wasn't the time. "Will do."

"Be careful." The words '*don't do anything stupid*' were implied, as usual.

Josh wasn't upset given the idiotic things he'd done under the influence. He'd lied enough about his drinking that no one trusted what he said these days, even though he was sober. His family wanted his actions to match his words, which he understood, but he was too far away to show them he was watching out for himself. His assurances would have to be enough for Sam. "I will be."

An hour later, Josh stopped by Sweet Caroline's Cafe for a tea, a coffee, and pastries—he'd asked if they knew Hope's favorites—they did—then he parked in front of a beach house twice the size of his cottage. She was waiting on the driveway with a large box next to her.

He pressed the button to open the trunk before sliding out of the car. "Nice place."

"It belongs to my brother." She wore white capris that hugged her hips, a blue T-shirt with an anchor emblem on the front, and a pair of white sandals. A navy tote bag hung off her shoulder. All she needed was a sailor hat to complete the nautical look.

Josh had to admit the outfit looked good on her. "The way you're dressed, we should be sailing to our destination."

"Yes, but we'd run aground as soon as we got started. We'll have to fly."

Hope picked up the box. "This should fit in your plane, but if not, we'll figure something else out. I told Dan to wrap the painting for shipping to protect it."

After she set the box in the trunk, Josh closed the hatch, circled to the passenger door, and opened it.

As surprise flashed in her eyes, he bit back a laugh. "Southern men aren't the only ones with manners."

"I didn't say anything," she said before getting into the car. A burst of strawberry surrounded him. Must be the scent of her shampoo or shower gel.

"You didn't have to." He kept his tone light. "Your eyes gave you away."

"I'm not used to it."

"A man being polite?"

She nodded. "The only guy I spend time with is my brother."

Josh hadn't expected such honesty. "No dates?"

"Nope." She fastened her seat belt and stared forward out the windshield.

He wanted to say more—ask why she didn't date—but he didn't want to spook her. Her stiff body language told him to tread carefully, and he would. This day was about helping others, not being a nosy busybody like the gossips back in Berry Lake.

He closed her door, went to the driver's side, and slid behind the steering wheel. "There's a caramel latte and an apple fritter for you."

She crossed her arms. "How did you know those are my favorites?"

"I asked." Josh pulled onto the road.

Hope's mouth quirked. "I'm not sure if that's a nice-guy move or creepy-stalker behavior."

"Nice guy all the way." He flashed his most charming smile, but she rolled her eyes. Yeah, today would be interesting. "If I hadn't asked, I would have gotten you what I'd ordered for myself."

"What's that?"

"Tea and a banana-walnut muffin."

She made a face. "Never mind. I'm glad you asked for my favorites."

"Permission to stalk, huh?"

"To keep me from eating anything with bananas? Yes."

"What's wrong with bananas?"

"They were my ex-husband's favorite." She shivered. "I can't stomach them now."

Ex-husband? That was unexpected, but knowing she'd been married shouldn't have surprised him. She was a pretty, smart, and kind woman, but Josh wondered what went wrong.

Maybe Hope wasn't quite the open book she appeared to be. Josh focused on the road. He couldn't wait to find out more about her.

* * *

This flight was a mistake. Hope sat in the right seat of Josh's jet while he took the left. She kept her hands on her right knee to keep it from bouncing. The way it had since they took off over thirty minutes ago.

Her nerves had skyrocketed the minute he'd shown up looking like a model from a photography shoot, and they hadn't settled. If anything, they'd gotten worse.

No man had the right to look that gorgeous in a pair of khakis and a button-up shirt—especially Josh Cooper. The short sleeves showed off his strong arms, too. She expected him to wear an expensive cologne, but the minty-woodsy mix of his soap was driving her crazy in the cockpit.

Yes, flying with him in the fanciest private plane she'd ever seen outside of the movies was a horrible idea. She couldn't think straight around Josh Cooper. That was why she'd mentioned Adam and his banana obsession.

Stupid.

But now sitting in this lightweight jet—whatever that meant—brought back bad memories of Adam's wealthy lifestyle. She'd never asked Josh what he did for a living. That was something that mattered to her ex, not to her. But seeing the luxurious cabin with four dark leather seats and a lavatory made her wonder how Josh afforded a plane like this.

He was attractive enough for Hollywood or New York, but she would recognize him if he were an actor or model. He'd said he lived in a small town. Did that make him a businessman or a trust-fund baby? If he were like Ashton Thorpe, the hero in Jenna Ford's thriller series, then Josh was a wealthy spy extraordinaire.

"What are you thinking about?" he asked.

He must be finished talking to air-traffic control and fiddling with the instrument panel. "You."

A pleased smile spread across his face. "What about me?"

"This is a nice plane. I was wondering if you're a professional pilot, wealthy spy, or a trust-fund baby."

"Three interesting professions."

"Are any close?"

"Not even warm."

Silence filled the cockpit. She wasn't having any of that. "Aren't you going to tell me?"

"What?" He feigned innocence.

"Your job."

He licked his lips slowly as if trying to draw the motion out as long as possible.

She watched for aesthetic value.

"No," he said. "I don't think I'll tell you."

"You're annoying."

"You thought so yesterday, too."

Hope did not have a poker face. "You're more annoying today, but no worries. I'll do an internet search when we land to get my answer."

A muscle twitched in his jaw. "I'm a football

commentator."

She didn't know if being a former athlete was a requirement but given his build, she assumed he might be one. "Radio or TV?"

"TV."

He had the looks for being in front of the camera, but that job must pay more than she thought to afford a plane like this.

"What's your favorite sport?"

"Does Olympic figure skating count? That's the extent of the sports I watch."

"I won't hold it against you." He didn't sound as if he cared, though he appeared to be holding back laughter. Then again, why should he care what sports she liked?

"Given you're stuck with me today, that's good."

"I appreciate your honesty. Some people might pretend to be a fan, but then say fourth period instead of the fourth quarter of a football game and lose credibility."

"Why would anyone do that?"

"To suck up."

"That's not me," she said quickly. "I don't even know what sport has periods."

"Hockey," he said without missing a beat. "There are three periods during regulation play. Football has four quarters."

"I know baseball has innings because my brother played."

"Twin brother, right?"

She nodded. "Von is less than three minutes older than me, but you'd think three years with the way he acts."

"Is he an artist like you?"

"Von remodels homes and sells them," she explained. "His work is so creative, but he'd never call himself an artist. He views what he does as only part of his job. But I think he's wrong."

Josh glanced her way. "Do you tell him that?"

"All the time."

"That doesn't surprise me."

She stuck her tongue out at him before laughing. "But seriously, he's the best brother ever. I don't know what I'd do without him."

"I feel the same about my sister and brother. We've gotten closer recently, and I wish it would have happened sooner."

The love for his family filled Hope with warmth. "Better late than never."

He nodded. "Football kept me away from home. Now we're figuring things out and getting along better than when we were kids."

"That's great." Even when she'd lived in New York, her and Von hadn't let the distance get in the way. She was grateful for that. "What do your brother and sister do?"

"Sam is my younger brother. He's a police officer in Seattle. My older sister, Ava, is a schoolteacher in our hometown."

"Honorable professions."

Josh nodded. "They're excellent at what they do."

Hope glanced around the cockpit. "You must be also to have a plane like this."

"I played football for eight seasons."

No wonder he could afford a jet like this. "Is that how you ended up a commentator?"

"Yes."

"I should have done an internet search on you before the flight, so I'd know more about you."

"I'm surprised you didn't."

She shrugged. "I had too much work to do last night. I'm not a big social media user."

"I'm burnt out on social media. On a hiatus for now."

"Does that mean you didn't run a search on me?"

"I didn't," he admitted, to her relief. "Did I miss anything good?"

"Nothing good." Thinking about the articles and posts regarding her canceled show and divorce knotted her stomach. As they flew above a smattering of clouds, she stared out of the window.

"Like your ex-husband?"

She jerked her gaze to Josh. "How'd you—"

"Lucky guess." He held up one of his hands. "You mentioned him earlier. I made an assumption."

"A correct one. Adam is temperamental, but he's respected and rich. Because of that, he gets away with a lot that others wouldn't." Hope would leave it at that. "At least that was how things were two years ago when I last saw him."

"I'm sorry things didn't work out."

"I'm not." She lowered her voice. "I'm better away from him."

"That's why they're called exes."

She nodded. "What about you?"

"No ex-husbands," he teased. "Or ex-wives. I've never been married."

"Once was enough for me."

"Until you meet the right guy?"

She shrugged. "Guess I'll have to see, but I'm of the mindset that happily ever after is a myth."

Hope wasn't planning on saying "I do" again, but only Paula and Von knew how she felt. Both said she'd change her mind, but she hadn't yet.

"I believe in happy endings, but you have to work for them," he said to Hope's surprise. "Nothing comes easy."

"I hope you find yours."

His gaze met hers. "Me, too."

More than a look passed between them. The connection sent her temperature soaring. Hope had never felt anything like that before. She wasn't sure she wanted to be feeling it now.

To break the contact, she turned her gaze out the side window. "It's peaceful flying."

"I love being up here."

"I see why." She didn't understand what was happening with Josh, but flying gave her a rare feeling of contentment. One she wanted to relish. "When I've flown before, I was rushing to get somewhere and wanted the flight to go by as quickly as possible. This isn't like that. It's so quiet."

"That's one reason I love flying. There's a calmness that's hard to replicate." He glanced at the instrument panel and then at her. "You can leave all your troubles down there and just be up here."

"I like it up here." She smiled at him. "I'm glad I got to see this side of flying."

And of him.

Maybe Josh wasn't as annoying as she thought.

7

On his descent into Nashville, Josh made the final preparations for landing. He and Hope were here to do a good deed, but he regretted the flight wasn't longer. He would have liked for them to keep talking and getting to know each other without another soul around. This space, this time, had been theirs alone, and he didn't want to give that up.

Josh glanced at Hope, who stared at the approaching runway with excitement. That reminded him they were here to pick up a painting. This wasn't a date.

The wheels touched down.

"Smooth landing," Hope said, seeming impressed.

"Now you'll know not to worry about the painting when we land back in Charleston."

"I wasn't worried." She didn't hesitate to answer.

His chest swelled with pride. Not because of the landing but due to her faith in him. One bad decision after another had brought him to this point in his life, but that path had led him to Hope. She was beautiful, inside and out. Trusting others didn't seem to come easy to her based on how she acted yesterday, yet he'd earned a bit of trust from her today. "Thanks."

He parked and then shut down the engines.

She unbuckled from her seat. "It didn't take us long to get here."

"That's because we talked most of the way." And joked and laughed. He liked how she didn't hold back with the town of Berry Lake's belief and use of Bigfoot to drive tourism. He might agree with her, but playing devil's advocate was more fun. Enjoying teasing her, he'd taken on the role of a Sasquatch believer.

"Well, you were right. Flying sure beats driving." She tucked several strands of hair behind her ears, scratched the back of her neck, and then wiped her hands over her pants. "What now?"

Her words broke the spell he'd been under watching her. "I have a couple of things to do if you want to move into the cabin."

"Sure." As she climbed out of her seat, he forced himself not to stare. "I'll get out of your way."

Another whiff of strawberry filled the air. He inhaled even though her scent was seared into his brain. Forget huckleberries—what Berry Lake was known for. Strawberries were his new favorite. When he smelled or ate one in the future, he had a feeling Hope Ryan would come to mind.

A few minutes later, Josh joined her in the cabin and picked up the box. "Did you hear from your friends?"

"Cami and Dan are at the hotel waiting for us." Hope held her cell. "I have the directions on my phone."

He motioned to the door. "Lead the way."

Yesterday, Hope had reminded him of Jenny, but the two women, both creative types, were more different than alike. Jenny had a quiet personality; Hope was more outgoing and didn't hesitate to ask questions or joke around. Jenny had been shy since elementary school, while Hope seemed subdued as if holding herself back.

That intrigued him.

So did her having an ex-husband.

A failed marriage might explain why she didn't date or believe in happily ever after. Josh hoped that wouldn't always be the case for her.

"We have to pick up the rental car I reserved," he said. "And then we'll be on our way."

As Josh drove into downtown Nashville, the robotic voice on Hope's phone kept them from getting lost. He parked at the front of the hotel where a man and woman in their late forties waved to them.

Hope leaned forward. "That's Cami and Dan."

The two wore shorts and T-shirts, but the dark circles under their eyes and pale faces suggested how difficult the past week had been for them.

Hope inhaled. "They look so sad."

"I'm sure you'll have them smiling in no time." She had that effect on him. Josh imagined she would on these two also.

She hurried out of the car, immediately hugging Cami. The woman gushed over her outfit and how sweet it was for Hope to travel all this way for the painting.

Introductions were made. The couple was friendly. They adored Hope as an artist and as a person also, given their praise. Josh felt as if he'd known them for years, not minutes, and understood Hope's desire to help them.

Dan retrieved the painting from the valet. It was wrapped up with two large foam sheets on either side. "I watched that video on how to package art."

Hope took the painting from him. "Looks perfect."

"He worked hard on that." Cami took a breath and then another. "I'm sorry your other four paintings were destroyed."

Hurt flashed across Hope's expression but then disappeared. If Josh hadn't been focused on her face, he wouldn't have noticed.

Cami wiped her eyes. "I don't know what you can do with this one—"

"I'll do everything I can." Hope's voice was

strong, yet full of compassion. Her name fit her perfectly at that moment, as she gave hope to Cami. "I've been in touch with two restoration services and the museum where I interned. I promise to do my best, but if I feel someone else can do a better job, I will let you know."

Josh's respect for her doubled. Not for her promise, but for her kindness toward this couple who had lost everything. Her selflessness impressed him, too. She had to be feeling a loss over those four paintings, but her concern had been only for Cami and Dan.

Josh had been wrong about Hope. He'd misjudged her, which made him feel like a bigger jerk. Even if she'd driven to Nashville and been exhausted, nothing would have stopped her from giving her all at Jenny and Dare's wedding. Hope had tried to tell him and Caroline that, but neither had listened. He owed Hope an apology.

"Thanks. We know you will, which is why we wanted to give the painting to you first." Emotion filled Cami's voice. "Take your time. There's no rush on this."

"We won't be back in the house for months."

A choked sob came from Cami. Dan put his arm around his wife, who sank into him as if exhausted. He stared at her like they were the only two people there. The love passing between them was palpable. It stole Josh's breath. He felt as though he were trespassing during an intimate moment, but he couldn't force his gaze away.

No woman had ever looked at him with so much love. A woman had never needed Josh to hold her and assure her everything would be okay. He'd never had a woman comfort him when everything was going wrong.

I want that.

I wish I had that now.

What would his life be like if he'd been in a loving relationship when he'd been injured? If he hadn't come out of that first surgery to find only his parents waiting by his bedside? If the love of his life had been holding his hand at night in the hospital instead of his brother or sister?

Not that he didn't need his family. He did. But would he have found the solace he'd needed through love instead of escaping into a haze of drunkenness? A woman like Hope would have the strength and compassion to see the man she loved through anything.

Unfortunately, he would have never looked twice at her until now. Before, he'd only dated models, actresses, singers, and other professional athletes. He'd wanted someone in his life who was well-known, who would be an asset to his career. It was why he'd asked out Jenny.

That was the kind of woman he thought would fit him and the life he'd wanted best. How wrong he'd been…

Hope held the box between her feet.

Josh hurried over to help her. He steadied the box. "This might make it easier."

She slid the painting inside with no problems. "Thanks."

"We make a good team." With that, he put the box carefully in the trunk.

"It's been a while since I've used oil paints. I'll need to practice first," she said to Cami and Dan. "I don't want to make any mistakes."

"We trust you," Dan said.

Hope smiled. "Thank you."

Cami hugged Hope. "If you start painting again, please let us know. We'd love to rebuild our collection with your works."

Hope didn't say anything, but Josh was confused. He'd seen the seascape panels hanging on the walls of the multipurpose room. She'd made Jenny and Dare's wedding favors. That meant Hope was still painting. Maybe he misunderstood what Cami meant.

"Thanks for bringing Hope to Nashville." Dan shook Josh's hand. "I miss seeing you throw the ball and scramble for those touchdowns."

Dan hadn't given any indication of recognizing Josh before, but he had, which meant he knew about this past year. Had Dan mentioned anything to Hope? If not, he probably would since they were friends.

Josh pulled at his collar. "Those were the days."

"Though I like hearing your game commentary.

You're one of the best announcers out there. Someday you might be better known for that than being a quarterback."

"Thanks." Josh appreciated the kind words, though he'd been a better quarterback than he was a commentator. "I'm looking forward to the upcoming season."

From the hotel, Josh drove to the barbeque restaurant. "Ready to buy me lunch?"

"All set." Hope patted her purse. "Order whatever you'd like."

"That could be dangerous."

"For my wallet, maybe, but I don't mind." She laughed, a sweet sound he wanted to hear again. "I brought my debit and credit cards with me."

As they walked inside, Josh placed his hand on Hope's back. She glanced over her shoulder at him with a soft smile. Guess touching her was okay. That pleased him.

A hostess seated them in a booth with red vinyl-covered benches and a wooden table with names and initials carved in the top. "Our family-style meals are the most popular. Your server will be with you shortly. Enjoy your barbeque.

Hope studied the menu. "Everything looks delicious."

"It is. The family style is the way to go if you want to try a variety of items."

"I do, so I'll let you order." She lowered her menu

to the table. "I'm not picky, and I have no food restrictions."

"Except bananas."

She nodded. "Oh, and anchovies."

"I'm sure we can work around those two," he joked.

"Josh Cooper." Their server, a man in his mid-twenties dressed in jeans and a red gingham shirt, bounded up with a huge grin on his face. "Man, it's been a long time since you were here. Too long."

"Hey, Russ." Josh shook hands with the restaurant owner's son. "I haven't made it back to town until now. I wanted my friend Hope to taste the best barbeque in Tennessee."

"You mean the entire South."

"Isn't that what I said?" Josh asked with a wink.

Russ's gaze turned serious. "Heard what happened last year. You doing better?"

"It's all good now." That wasn't the entire truth, but things were on the upswing. Josh pointedly eyed Hope to stop Russ from saying anymore. "What would you like to drink?"

"Strawberry lemonade."

"Make that two," he said to Russ.

"Coming right up." Russ shook his head. "Dad will be upset he missed you."

"I'll be back if we're scheduled for a game here."

"That might take away some of the sting," Russ said. "You're one of his favorite players."

With that, Russ turned to go put in their drink orders.

Hope studied Josh as if he were a rare lab specimen. "People recognize you when you go out."

Her statement didn't surprise him or put him off. "Football fans sometimes do. It started in college when we won a bowl game. After I was drafted in the first round, things got crazier."

"I'm assuming first round means you're good."

"I was." All-pro, MVP, offensive player of the year—the accolades and awards streamed through his brain. "Until I was tackled during a game and broke my leg. I had a few surgeries, but it was clear I would never again play the way I did, so I retired."

Those brief sentences didn't come close to what he'd gone through while on pain medication, trying to get through the day. No one would talk about his future in football, even though it had been all he wanted to know. Waiting to find out his prognosis had been agonizing.

"Not being able to play any longer hit me hard. Decimated me. I was a football player, a quarterback, then suddenly I wasn't anymore. I didn't know who I was without the game." The words came from deep inside him. He wasn't sure why they'd picked now to appear. He would have preferred they remained buried.

"I'm sorry." She reached across the table, sliding her hand into his. Heat flowed from her to him.

Comfort, too. He got a glimpse of what Cami and Dan must feel. That only made Josh want it more.

"Having what you love to do ripped away from you feels like a part of you has died." Hope's words came out fast. "As you said, you don't know who you are with that gone, and you're left to figure it out when pieces of your heart are missing."

"Exactly." So-called friends had told Josh to stop complaining because he had enough money to never work again, but football had been his life. Without the game, he was nothing. Each day had gotten harder. Only one thing had dulled that emptiness and bitterness—alcohol.

"I was living in a nightmare that wouldn't end," he admitted.

Nodding, she squeezed his hand. "You want to wake up, but you are awake. Nothing you do feels like it will change anything. You're out of control, and the future looks bleak."

"It was so frustrating."

"An effort in futility," she agreed.

Josh had never connected with someone as fast as he had with Hope. Her understanding hadn't just come to her. Either she'd had a similar experience or known someone who had. He wanted to know which one.

Dare he ask?

They were getting to know each other, and he didn't want her to retreat. That might happen if he pushed her too hard. Yet, he couldn't deny something drew them together. He glanced at their linked hands. Maybe this would bring them closer.

"Did something like that happen to you?" he asked.

8

As Josh's question swirled through Hope's mind, her muscles tensed. She pulled her arm back because her fingers trembled when she was stressed. That was the only way to describe how she felt at the moment.

"If you don't want to answer, that's fine," Josh said. "But I haven't met many people who've been through something similar."

"I understand." And she did. "This isn't a big secret. Most people in Indigo Bay know, but talking about it…"

"Is hard," he finished for her.

Oh so hard. But if she didn't tell Josh, an internet search or someone in town would. She wanted him to know her side of the story—the truth.

Besides, he'd been through this himself. Not the

same situation but close enough. He wouldn't judge her as others had.

Ignoring her tense body, she made herself sit taller. "Since my divorce, I haven't painted any works like the one we picked up today. I've tried, gone to counseling, tried again. But the canvas remains blank no matter what I do."

Realization dawned on his face. "That's what Cami meant about you painting."

Hope hadn't known if Josh had heard that or not. Guess so.

She nodded. "It's been two years."

"I'm sorry," he said.

"It is what it is." She'd accepted not being able to paint as she once had. That was the only way to keep from being consumed by bitterness over Adam's betrayal. "Fortunately, I'm able to paint in different ways from before and still earn a living selling those pieces."

"You figured a way to keep your passion for art alive and a part of your life." His gaze—full of understanding—met hers. "That's why I took the broadcaster job."

She never thought they'd have so much in common. "I have, but…"

"What?"

A stone settled in her stomach. "I'm scared I won't be able to repair the painting, but I have to try, even if I disappoint Cami and Dan."

"You'll do it." His conviction surprised her. "Cami and Dan believe in you. So do I."

Hope appreciated his words—needed them—but she had to ask. "We hardly know each other. Why are you so certain I can do this?"

"You want to help others. That's why you're here today. To do what you can for Cami and Dan. Restoring their piece might be what you need to heal from whatever is keeping you from painting. A spark will ignite that passion again."

If only... "I would love that, but I've been disappointed before. I'm not holding my breath."

"Well, if you were holding your breath, you'd turn blue or pass out. It's good you aren't."

That made her smile. Hope liked how she and Josh could talk about serious things, yet he'd add a dash of humor to keep things from getting too heavy.

Russ delivered their strawberry lemonades and two straws. "Did you know what you want to eat?"

"The Junior Platter for two," Josh said.

Russ picked up the menus. "Excellent choice. I'll get your order right in."

"Thanks." As soon as Russ was gone, Josh leaned forward, his gaze intent on her. "Full disclosure, I'm ready to go into busybody listening mode if you feel like telling me what happened with your divorce."

A few people had tried to get her to share juicy details others didn't know, but Hope found his honesty refreshing.

She unwrapped her straw, then stuck it in her glass. "Adam Darby, my ex-husband, is well-known in the art world. I met him at an exhibit when I was twenty-two. He became my manager and then my boyfriend. Three months later, we married. His connections gave me opportunities most artists only dream about. It helped that people liked my work, but I can't deny the role Adam played in my success."

As Josh sipped his drink, Hope tore the straw wrapper into tiny pieces.

"We'd been married for four years when the biggest show of my career was coming up. Some pieces were at the gallery, but most were still in my studio at our loft. Adam had set up an interview for me. During it, I talked about being married to my manager and wanting to have kids. The day after the interview went live, another artist he represented came to see me. She arrived at my door in tears, saying Adam had told her we were getting a divorce. That he was going to marry her. Turns out they'd been having an affair for months. The news blindsided me. I'd been working so hard on the show I had no idea."

Josh rubbed his chin. "I can't imagine the shock."

"I was hurt and numb at the same time. I wish I could say I instantly knew what I would do, but I'd be lying. I loved him. I truly believed he loved me."

With a trembling hand, Hope raised her glass and sipped.

Josh slid out of his side of the booth, scooted next

to Hope, and placed his arm around her. "Since you are busy destroying the straw wrapper, I can't hold your hand like you did mine. I figured this was the next best way to comfort you."

"Works for me." His strong, warm body made her feel safe. "That night, I confronted Adam at our loft. I was angry, but he was perfectly calm. I guess he'd been expecting a confrontation and was ready. He blamed me for his affair—said I wasn't giving him the attention he needed. He told me he forgave me for ignoring him, and he wanted to make our marriage work. He thought attending couple's counseling would help us move forward."

Josh's mouth gaped. "The guy had nerve."

"Adam is charismatic and used to getting his way. He didn't think this would be any different." She raised her chin. "I told him I wanted a divorce because there was no way I could stay married to him, knowing he'd been lying all these months and blaming me for what he'd done. He was livid I would consider leaving him. His ego was that big. He wanted both a wife and a mistress. I said no, and he threatened to destroy me before he would let me go. Usually, I could calm him down when he was upset, but not that time. I left and stayed with two of our friends at their place. The next day, I went back to the apartment. My friends came with me. And…"

Josh gave her a squeeze. "You don't have to keep going."

"It's okay." She wanted to continue. "The more times I tell it, the less power what happened has on me. At least that's what a counselor told me."

But she hadn't talked about this to anyone in a while. It would be good to gauge her reaction to telling this story again.

"The loft looked as if a hurricane had ripped through it. My clothes had been shredded. Everything of mine was destroyed, including all the pieces for the show."

Josh's nostrils flared. His face reddened. "Hope…"

"This was two years ago. It's not worth getting angry over."

"You're worth it."

Her heart bumped. "Thanks. My biggest mistake was returning to the apartment without the police. Adam paid off my two so-called friends to back up his claim I'd done the damage in a drunken, jealous fit over his affair. He'd placed empty bottles of alcohol all over the apartment, which was weird because we only drank wine, but that must have been part of his plan to ruin me."

"No wonder you don't like bananas."

Hope's mouth slanted. "You have no idea."

As she sipped her lemonade, her hand was steady. Progress.

"While I was at the apartment that morning, he was with his attorney planning to file for a divorce before I could. He described me as a psychotic, scorned woman who destroyed a dozen of her own paintings and their loft."

Josh swore under his breath. "I know a guy who knows a guy…"

"Two years ago, I may have taken you up on that, but Adam Darby isn't worth the effort or the jail time." Josh hadn't loosened his hold on her. If anything, he held her closer, and she found strength in his nearness. "Everyone we knew—and strangers, too—believed his lies. I went from being a beloved up-and-coming artist to a pariah. His lover somehow convinced him to get the gallery to let her take over my show. By then, Von had driven up to help me try to salvage what we could from the loft. After I returned to Indigo Bay, I thought painting would help me heal, but I couldn't. Every time I tried, I saw those broken frames and ripped canvases. All those months of work… gone."

"That's understandable."

"I've done therapy, weekend workshops, hypnosis, but that part of my creativity isn't there anymore."

"Unless it's hibernating."

"Time to wake up if that's the case. Two springs have passed."

"If it's any consolation, being in the broadcast booth kept me in football, but that wasn't enough to stop the regrets and bitterness from getting the worst of me. The only thing that helped was drinking."

"Oh, Josh. I'm so sorry." She sank against him, but he didn't seem to mind. "We are quite the pair, aren't we?"

He rubbed her arm. "I told you we made a good team. We can support and help each other."

Hope nodded. "That would be great. The worst part about not painting is I feel like I'm allowing Adam to win."

"You won by getting away from him."

A smile tugged at her lips. "That's what my brother says."

"He's right," Josh said. "You went through so much, and you may have tried to go back to painting too soon. Maybe you should try again."

"Unfortunately, the urge to paint isn't there. Before, I couldn't stop myself from working on a project, but now… nothing. Maybe I need more time."

"See what happens with the restoration first, but your ex deserves whatever bad karma comes his way."

"I try not to think about him."

"Smart." Josh dropped his gaze to the table. "I'm sorry I brought him up."

"Hey, it's okay. You didn't force me to talk. I wanted to tell you what happened." Hope wasn't upset at all. "If you'd done an internet search, the results would make you think I was an insane artist who should be avoided at all costs."

His face fell. After loosening his arm from around her, he leaned away.

She had no idea what was going on or why he'd shut down. "Are you okay?"

"I need to tell you what you would have found if you'd searched me. The drinking I mentioned…" He dragged his hand over his face. "I'm a recovering alcoholic who was arrested in July for threatening a barista, spent three months in rehab, and am on a medical leave of absence from the network while I get sober."

"Oh, Josh. You've gone through so much."

Not being able to paint seemed minor compared to what could have happened to her if she hadn't had Von around to take care of her. It was her turn to reach out to him.

She angled toward him, reaching to touch his arm. "How's your recovery going?"

"I'm heading toward my eleventh month of being sober."

"That's great, but I imagine it's been a rough time."

"Rough isn't always a bad thing," he admitted. "Getting drunk was easy; staying sober is difficult but worth it."

"We haven't known each other long, but I'm proud of you."

"Right back at you." He winked. "But I still might have to do an internet search on you to see how cray-cray your jerk of an ex made you out to be."

Laughing after a serious conversation wasn't what

she expected to be doing, but it felt good. Right. The same way being with Josh felt.

"Looks like the two of you are having a good time." Russ and another server, wearing a similar outfit, arrived with two trays full of meat, sides, plates, and utensils. "Enjoy your Junior Platter."

Hope stared in awe at the table filled with baked beans, fried okra, coleslaw, potato wedges, cornbread, and a platter of brisket, ribs, and chicken. "There's enough to feed eight people and still have leftovers to take home."

"Then it's a good thing we're not in a hurry, and I have a fridge in the plane." He raised his glass of lemonade. "To delicious food and new friends."

Feeling an unfamiliar sense of contentment, she tapped her glass against his. "You can never have enough of either. Especially friends."

* * *

That afternoon, Josh stood behind Hope on her front porch as she dug through her purse for her keys. He held onto the box with the painting even though Hope could have carried it herself. Truth was after such a great day, he wasn't ready to say goodbye.

He'd rather take off with her again. Fly around so they could spend more time together with zero interference from phone calls, texts, waiters, or fans. So far, they'd talked about their families, college, her painting, and his broadcasting, but he wanted to learn more about Hope.

Who was he kidding?

He wanted to know everything about her.

She glanced over her shoulder "My keys are in here somewhere."

"I'm in no rush." The alternative was being alone. He'd rather stay here with Hope as long as possible.

Metal clanked together.

"Here they are." She unlocked the front door, then pushed it open. "My studio is down the hallway."

Josh stepped inside, eyes widening. He felt as if he'd stepped onto a set for a home decorating show. From the vaulted beam ceiling to the wide plank flooring to the comfortable couch against the wall, everything fit together. Comfortable and homey. He whistled. "I thought the house looked great on the outside, but the interior is amazing."

"This was one of my brother's first remodels and his first attempt at an open-floor plan." She spoke with pride. "Von says he wants to redo the house, but I keep telling him you can't improve upon perfection."

"He nailed it."

Josh followed her down the hallway to her studio. The room was large with tiled floors. Sunlight streamed through the windows and a set of French doors that led to a deck in the back. The ocean view was breathtaking.

"This studio has everything you need," he said.

"Von went a little crazy, but he was happy to have me home."

Josh could only imagine her brother's relief. "My sister likes me being in Berry Lake. My brother is happy I'm closer to him, too."

A coat rack held two pairs of stained coveralls.

He walked toward a built-in unit of cabinets, countertop, and shelving along the side wall. A steel laundry sink was empty. Magnets painted with pretty beach scenes, including a few of the gazebo he'd seen when he arrived, and the words Indigo Bay written in cursive at the bottom covered the counter.

Everything seemed to have its place. He was more of a find-a-place-where-it-fits kind of guy. "Is your studio always this clean?"

"I wish." She laughed—the melodic sound filled an empty place inside Josh. "This is much cleaner than I usually leave it."

"So you're not a neat freak?"

She laughed. "Not even close. I try not to let the mess get out of control, but often my hands and clothes have as much paint on them as what I'm working on."

"Occupational hazard."

Nodding, she opened a closet door. "The painting can go in here."

Josh set the box inside, and then he looked around the studio. A few sketches of the beach hung on a corkboard. A large box on the floor contained tin buckets wrapped in cellophane and tied with white and purple ribbons.

No paintings or blank canvases anywhere. This was set up more like his mom's craft room than a studio, except for an empty easel in the far corner next to folded drop cloths.

Hope seemed to have accepted whatever was keeping her from painting and moved on. He wished he'd been able to do that after his injury.

"This is a great space," he said.

Her lips curved into a satisfied smile. "It used to be a third bedroom."

Josh made his way over to the French doors, whistling under his breath. "The views are incredible."

"It's one of my favorite things about this house." She stared at the water. "In the morning, I sit on the deck and have a cup of coffee. It's the perfect start to my day."

"Mind if I go outside?"

"Please do." She followed him out the doors and onto the deck.

He placed his hands on the railing, taking a deep breath. "I might be able to get used to the heat and humidity with a deck like this."

Hope stood next to him. Even though hours had passed, she still smelled like strawberries. "Having a breeze like today helps."

The wind tousled the ends of her hair, blowing strands across her face. Josh reached to brush them aside for her. "Now you can see better."

Her lips parted as if surprised, but she didn't back away from him. "Thanks."

Josh couldn't stop staring at those lips. He wanted a taste. "Is it okay if I kiss you?"

A slight nod was the only invitation he needed.

Lowering his head, he pressed his lips against hers. Gently. Tentatively.

His lips moved over hers, testing and tasting.

He hadn't kissed anyone in months, but he didn't remember anything ever feeling so right the first time. As if he'd found what he hadn't known was missing.

He increased the pressure against her mouth. As she leaned against him, he wrapped his arms around her, pulling her closer. The kiss deepened. She clung to him.

The warmth turned into heat.

Need built, and his control slipped.

Stop.

But he didn't want to.

He needed this. Needed her. Needed more…

9

Josh Cooper was kissing her. Hope was kissing him back, too. She wasn't sure how this had happened or why, but she didn't care. Not when tingles lit up her body from having his lips on hers.

Hunger driving her, she arched to get closer to him.

He was strong and warm. His hands rubbed her back, sending pleasurable sensations shooting throughout her body.

Kissing him wasn't something she'd planned on or even considered, but she hoped he didn't stop.

From his amazing minty, woody scent to the hard muscles beneath her palms, Josh called to her. All day, his words and accidental touches chipped away at the wall she'd built around her heart, putting cracks into a barrier she'd believed impenetrable. But his lips might as well be a battering ram. His kisses were melting her resolve, her…everything.

She'd forgotten how good being kissed felt—the connection, the warmth, the sensations—but she didn't remember it ever feeling this good, as if his lips had been made for her.

"Hope…" He whispered her name between kisses before pulling back slightly. His lips look puffy, the way hers felt. "I want to keep kissing you, but if I do, I'm not going to want to stop."

Oh, no. What was she doing?

He'd asked first, and she'd agreed, but they were friends, right? Friends didn't kiss. Not like this.

Heart pounding, Hope took a step back, turned away from him, and brought trembling fingers to her throbbing lips. She could count the number of men she'd kissed on one hand. Kissing with such abandon wasn't like her.

"Hope?" Josh sounded out of breath, but she didn't dare face him after she'd kissed him back with such abandon. "I'm sorry… I-I got carried away."

"Me, too." Heat rushed up her neck.

The worst part? She wouldn't mind another kiss. That shocked her. Not wanting to date should imply a disinterest in kissing, but apparently, her warm-all-over body that wanted his lips plastered against hers again hadn't gotten that memo.

Tension crackled between them. Waves broke against the sand, echoing the turmoil inside her. The

Melissa McClone

lack of conversation was uncomfortable. Unsure what to say or do next, she stared at the water.

"Kissing me freaked you out," Josh said. It wasn't a question.

"A little. Okay, a lot." She didn't know how he'd figured that out when they hadn't known each other long. "The kiss was… nice."

"Nice?"

"Hot," she tried instead.

"That's better." He cupped her chin, tipping her face toward his. "What are you thinking?"

"You're the first man I've kissed since my divorce." She couldn't believe she'd allowed Josh to kiss her. Not with her trust issues, yet this hadn't felt wrong. "I wasn't sure if I'd remember how."

Oh, no. Had she said that aloud?

Heat burned her cheeks.

Hope fought the urge to run off the deck and bury her head in the sand. Instead, she tried to turn away from Josh, but he wouldn't let her.

"You remembered well." As his thumb caressed her jawline, he smiled. "You're my first kiss since I entered rehab in July."

"A day of firsts."

He inclined his head. "You mentioned not dating earlier."

She nodded. "I'm over Adam. So over him, but I've never been one to date for the sake of going out. I'm not looking for a relationship, so…"

"I've only dated casually in the past. Relationships and getting sober aren't the best combo, but there's nothing wrong with hanging out."

"Hanging out?"

"Like we did today," he explained.

"What about kissing?"

His blue eyes twinkled. "The timing seemed right for one."

"It was." The kiss had been perfect, one of the top ten things she'd done this year. But one kiss didn't mean anything, even if her lips might disagree.

"We'll have to see if the timing is right for another. I'm only here until Sunday, but I want to spend more time with you."

Josh was easy to talk to. He understood what she'd gone through with her painting better than most. He also kissed like a dream, even if she didn't know whether they'd do that again. "I'd like that, too."

"Great." His grin crinkled the corners of his eyes. Man, he was gorgeous. "I'm going to a support meeting tonight, but I'd love to check out Indigo Bay tomorrow if you'd like to play tour guide."

"I'd be happy to show you around my hometown."

"I'll text you in the morning after my run. That's how I begin my day."

"Yours sounds healthier than mine." And more eye appealing as she imagined him in a pair of shorts and running shoes, with no shirt. "If you run this far, maybe we'll start our days together."

Oops. The idea sounded better in her head, but nothing she could do about that now.

"I might have to do that." His tone wasn't flirtatious or suggestive but…playful.

She hoped he would.

Warning lights flashed in her head. Hope didn't date. She didn't want to date. Except her usual self-preservation wasn't kicking in. She wanted to see Josh again. Not tomorrow sightseeing or Friday at the wedding when she'd be working, but tomorrow morning, the two of them out here alone again.

Friends or… more?

Wait. She couldn't let herself get carried away due to a kiss. Josh was leaving in a few days. There wasn't the possibility of something more.

So why were her lips still tingling?

She didn't know the answer, but surprisingly, the question didn't frighten Hope as much as it should have.

* * *

Normally, a morning run prepared Josh for the day ahead. Not today. He struggled to keep moving. Maybe later when he could check in with his family, he'd have more energy because he didn't want to worry them.

As the waves rolled in, he jogged along the wet sand. His pace was slower than usual due to tiredness, but also because running at his usual speed made no sense when he'd be touring the town later. His leg could only take so much.

A gull flew overhead. Josh dreamed of having freedom again, but his life was all about accountability these days. What he deserved, but he doubted teenagers received as many texts and calls from their parents as Josh did.

He yawned.

Sleep hadn't come easy. He'd tossed and turned, thinking about kissing Hope. He'd meant to brush his lips over hers, not linger until the kiss turned hot and heavy.

Which it had.

Boiling.

That was why he'd pulled back. Things were getting out of control. He wanted to blame his reaction on thinking about having a woman in his life or on not being physical with anyone in almost a year, but neither was the case. The reason was Hope herself. He'd never connected as deeply to another person as he had with her. He wanted to kiss her again, see if he had the same response. He hoped he'd get the chance today.

A Golden Retriever chased after something in the water. The dog splashed through the waves before dashing back to the sand with a ball in its mouth.

Josh jogged down the beach. As he came closer to Hope's house, he saw her sitting on a chair. Sunglasses rested on the top of her head. She wore a pair of shorts and an oversized sweater with the sleeves rolled up.

Something fluttered in his stomach.

Hunger. He hadn't eaten anything because he was meeting Hope at Sweet Caroline's Cafe.

He squinted to get a better look at her.

The steaming mug on the table seemed all but forgotten as she flicked her gaze from the water to the notebook on her lap, her pencil moving across the paper as she did. The next time she looked up, he waved.

A smile lit up her pretty face. "Good morning. Enjoying your run?"

"It's more of a jog, but I am." Especially now he'd seen her. "Are you drawing something?"

"It's a sketch for wedding favors." She placed her notebook and pencil on the table, and then picked up her coffee. "I have to send the bride and groom ideas next week."

"You work ahead."

"I have a schedule worked out. That way, I have time for commissions, events at the resort, and the Indigo Bay-themed items I sell."

He marched in place to keep his heart rate up, but he wasn't ready to jog away. "You mentioned ornaments, and I saw the magnets. What else do you make?"

"Pins, bottles, tin buckets. Anything tourists might want to take home to remind them of their vacation."

As she stood and walked to the rail, Josh tried not

to stare at her long legs. He dropped his gaze to her toenails—painted a sparkly purple. Interesting. She didn't seem like the glitter type.

"I'll have to get something for my mom and sister."

"I'm sure it's the same type of items you'd find in Berry Lake."

"You make Bigfoot keychains, too?"

She rolled her eyes, but the laughter in her gaze kicked up his pulse. Or maybe that was from marching.

"I learned how to work with glass last fall," she added. "I'll go back to that after the wedding season ends and see what new items I can create."

No paintings were mentioned, but he understood why.

"Give watercolors a try. Those would make great postcards." A man exited the French doors of the studio, joining Hope on the deck. He had the same eyes and hair color as Hope, but he was five inches taller and all muscle. The guy eyed Josh suspiciously. "Who's your friend?"

Hope sighed. "Josh, this is my brother Von. Von, this is Josh Cooper."

"Nice to meet you," Josh said. "You have a great house."

Von's jaw jutted forward. "You're the quarterback turned sports announcer."

The distrustful tone suggested Von recognized Josh and was overprotective of his sister.

"That's me," Josh replied. What else could he say? Her brother knew who he was, which meant he likely knew about his past.

"How do you know each other?" Von's gaze bounced from Hope to Josh.

Interesting. Hope must not have told her brother who flew her to Nashville.

"We met in the multipurpose room at the cottages on Tuesday," Hope said before he could reply. "Josh delivered that thank-you gift from the bride getting married on Friday. You borrowed the autographed book, remember?"

Von didn't say anything.

Josh didn't mind taking up the slack. "Jenny texted last night. She's in town and loves the resort. I mentioned the panels you painted. She can't wait to see them."

Hope's shoulders shimmied. "I hope she likes them and everything else."

"She will." Josh liked seeing Hope excited. "Jenny is meeting with Zoe today."

Von rubbed his chin. "How long are you in town for, Josh?"

"Until Sunday." He wouldn't be surprised if the guy brought out a knife to sharpen or a gun to clean. Von had a marking-my-territory-stay-away-from-my-sister gleam in his eyes.

"Josh is from a small town in Washington state," Hope said. "They host a Bigfoot Seekers Gathering each year."

Von laughed. "This is why we live on the East Coast away from all the crazies."

As Hope's gaze met Josh's, a look passed between them and then a smile. He knew she was thinking about their conversation yesterday, the same as him.

Their shared glance didn't go unnoticed by her brother. Von's frown deepened.

"Time for me to head back. Nice meeting you, Von." Josh nodded at Hope. "See you at nine."

She grinned. "Looking forward to it."

"What's going on at nine?" Von asked.

"We're having breakfast." She turned toward her brother. "Then I'm giving Josh a tour of Indigo Bay. Any other questions?"

Von started to say something, but then pressed his lips together.

Josh understood. Von was likely trying to protect his sister.

"I'm not in town long, and my younger brother's vacation didn't get approved." Josh wanted to put Von at ease. "I'm glad your sister's willing to show me around, or I'd be doing it on my own."

Von's hard expression didn't change, but Josh had done what he could. Still, he understood why her brother was acting this way.

Josh had made mistakes. Big ones. Some the public knew about.

Not repeating those was better than the

alternative—drinking himself stupid until he ended up hurting himself or someone else. He almost had with Jenny. There wouldn't be a next time.

He'd led a lonely, miserable life since his injury. Learning about himself, making changes, and getting sober this past year had given him a second chance to be the man he wanted to be—healthy, worthy, loved…

As Josh stared at Hope, a longing unfurled in his heart.

Would he ever be the kind of man a woman like her would want?

* * *

As soon as Josh jogged away, Hope glared at Von. She couldn't believe him. Talking to Josh had been great until her brother showed up. "Why were you rude to Josh?"

Her brother's nostrils flared. "Why are you all buddy-buddy with that drunk loser?"

Unbelievable. She squared her shoulders.

Hope loved Von. She didn't want to fight about this, but the way he acted was embarrassing. "Josh is a recovering alcoholic. He went to rehab and is sober."

"For now." Her brother's vitriol surprised her. "Cooper might be a future Hall of Famer, but even before his injury, he was nothing but bad news. He'll break your heart."

"We hardly know each other." And shared a hot

kiss, but who knew if that would happen again.

"You don't follow football. You have no idea what Josh Cooper is like." Von joined her at the railing. "He's a total player. Always has been. He uses women and then dumps them. One after another."

"Josh hasn't dated anyone since he went into rehab."

"Until you."

"We're hanging out," she countered with no hesitation. "It's no big deal."

Von rolled his eyes. "He's the first man you've spent time with since Adam. This is a bigger deal than you're making it."

"Yesterday, we spent the day together and got to know each other. I realized how little fun I have in my life. Even when I lived in New York, Adam decided what we did. In the four years I was with him, I don't remember joking around and laughing until I cried."

"That happened with Josh?" Suspicion laced each of her brother's words.

Hope raised her chin. She wouldn't back down over this. "Yes, and I enjoyed myself."

Telling Josh what had happened with Adam hadn't been easy. Few had heard her side of the story, but her counselor had been right about not being afraid to talk about it. Yesterday, Hope had taken a huge step forward after only brief feelings of angst surfaced. No tears, either. Instead of feeling ashamed, she'd discussed the nightmare end of her marriage, laughed, and ate way too much food. Both Von and Paula would be shocked. Hope had been but pleased, too.

"I hope we have as good a time today," she added.

"He's still bad news, sis."

She disagreed. Everything Josh did showed her a man who wanted to change his life and was doing that. "Your 'bad news' guy flew the bride's wedding dress across the country, and he delivered her thank-you gifts. He flew me to Nashville to pick up that painting. Last night, he went to a sobriety meeting while on vacation on the other side of the country. That shows how serious he is about staying sober. Someone's past shouldn't define him. I'm willing to give Josh the benefit of the doubt. What I hope others give me. That's what friends do."

"You're defending the guy like you're his champion."

"You did the same with me." Hope hated when people wrongly judged her by Adam's lies. She wouldn't do the same to Josh. "I'm paying it forward."

"Okay, you got me. I'm judging Josh on the same kind of rumors that ruined your reputation." Von's expression was contrite. "But you like him."

"He's a nice guy."

"Nothing else?"

Other than him being the most attractive guy she'd ever seen and crush-worthy, but Von didn't need to know that. "No."

"Okay, but make sure being friends—" He used

two of his fingers on each hand to put imaginary quote marks around the last word. "—doesn't morph into something else."

Hope groaned. "Even if it did, which it won't, he's leaving on Sunday."

"Adam swept you away before any of us knew what was going on."

"I was fresh out of college. Young. Naïve." And totally overwhelmed by the well-known manager's attention. He was handsome, charming, and wealthy. He'd built her up. Each compliment made her believe she couldn't fail, but somehow at the same time, he'd convinced she needed him to succeed. "I'm not the same as I was then."

"You may not want to date now, but somewhere inside you is that little girl who drew castles and dreamed of her own happily ever after. You're not as trusting as you were, but you still have a pure heart." Von's gaze softened. "I don't want another guy to break you the way Adam did. I worried I might lose you forever. That's why I'm not welcoming Josh Cooper with open arms. Any man who enters your life, even as a friend, will have to prove himself worthy of you."

Whatever anger she'd felt dissolved. She couldn't be mad at her brother for loving her so much. "Okay, you're forgiven, but please be nicer if you see Josh again."

"I will, but you need to promise me you'll be

careful around him."

"Nothing's going to—"

"Promise me, sis."

She sighed. The worst thing that would come of spending time with Josh would be a crush—which she probably had already. That she could handle. Still, if it made Von happy... "I promise."

10

Hope was having as much fun sightseeing in her hometown with Josh as she did flying to Nashville. No serious topics had come up like yesterday. Today was about enjoying themselves, joking and laughing as they made their way around Indigo Bay.

She could have done without other women blatantly checking Josh out. If he noticed, he didn't let on nor did he flirt back. Honestly, she didn't blame them. He was gorgeous and dressed for the beach. His bright board shorts brought to mind sunsets streaked with reds hinting of a storm brewing. His vibrant orange T-shirt showed off his tan and white straight teeth.

But his easy smile was what called to Hope the most. A happy face beat a handsome one any day of the week. Josh also seemed more relaxed today. She hoped that meant he was enjoying sightseeing with her.

Two people exited Happy Paws Pet Shop. The man and woman held hands and gazed lovingly into each other's eyes.

Her ribs squeezed tight. She tried not to stare at the pair, to focus on the display in the nearest window, or to look at Josh, but something about these two brought back a rush of memories from her four-year marriage that she'd pushed aside to get over Adam's betrayal.

The couple's arms formed a V with their linked hands and swung back and forth playfully.

Pleasant times with her ex-husband flashed in her brain like a strobe light. A dinner at a rooftop restaurant, watching a parade, strolling through Central Park, cuddling during a movie marathon at their neighborhood cinema.

Had the end been horrible? Yes, but Hope realized she'd been so focused on the bad things she'd forgotten the good times in her marriage. She missed feeling cherished and respected. Missed having someone to share the ups and downs with and to depend on. Missed hearing the words *I love you.*

Not that she wanted to fall in love again. But she recognized the appeal of being in a relationship. Not everything had been negative.

A lightness spread through her. This was a positive step. Hope had Josh to thank for that.

He sauntered beside her with a wide grin on his face, a baseball cap on his head, and sunglasses covering his eyes. No one had recognized him yet.

"Of all the shops we've been to," Josh said, "the Chocolate Emporium is my favorite."

"You can never go wrong with chocolate."

"My second favorite is the art gallery," he added.

That surprised her. "I didn't realize you were into art."

"Art is hit or miss with me," he replied honestly. "But I like the ornaments they carry."

Hers were the only ones sold there. Warmth radiated deep inside her. She'd tried hard to continue her work as an artist. Ornaments were her favorite to make. The various surfaces and shapes often required extra creativity. Plus, she loved adding to someone's tradition whether that was buying an ornament from places they'd visited or having a piece be a part of a family's holiday decorating.

She swallowed around the emotion thickening her throat. "That's sweet of you to say."

"It's the truth. I put five on hold," he said, rendering her speechless at the gesture. "One for each member of my family."

Wait. That didn't sound right. After clearing her throat, she said, "But you only need four to give to your family."

Josh grinned as if he had a secret. "One's for me."

Her pulse had been racing off and on all day, but

now it was in a full-on sprint.

Josh grabbed her hand, yanking her hard against him. "Watch out."

A kid on a scooter barreled past them.

Tingles erupted where his fingers touched hers. Heat, too. She stood so close she could hear him breathe, faster and faster. The tourists around them faded into the background. The only thing she saw was Josh.

He licked his lips. "That was close."

She agreed, realizing he was still holding her hand. One of his arms had slipped around her waist at some point.

"You okay?" he asked.

Hope had no idea what she was feeling other than the certainty she'd be happy to stand here with him all day. Being this close to him made her feel whole, a way she hadn't felt since returning to Indigo Bay.

You need to promise me you'll be careful around him.

She hadn't needed to be careful around Josh until now. Her brother had been correct when he'd said she'd almost lost her entire self, not only her painting, after what happened with Adam. She couldn't chance that happening again, but she wasn't ready to back away from Josh yet.

Something was happening to her, but she didn't know what.

His gaze searched hers. "Hungry?"

For a kiss. She gulped. That probably wasn't what he had in mind.

Hope nodded. "It has to be close to one o'clock. Let's grab lunch and eat down at the shore."

After a stop at the burger joint for a to-go order, Hope sat next to Josh on a bench overlooking the beach. He sipped his milkshake while she separated out their burgers and fries. "Food with a view."

He placed his drink on the ground, then took his share when she handed it to him. "Can't beat this."

"Nope." The Atlantic wasn't the only breathtaking sight with Josh next to her.

That explained the butterflies in her stomach, and why she wanted to scoot closer to him until their legs touched. Not that she had or would. But she'd thought about it—twice.

If her heart wasn't off the market; if he didn't live on the opposite side of the country; if he wasn't out of her league… she'd ask him to join her for dinner tonight. But the number of *ifs* told her appreciating him from afar was the safer option. Von would agree.

See, she could be careful.

"Great burger," he said in between bites. "Hits the spot."

A drop of ketchup rested on the side of his mouth. She wiped it off with a napkin. "There."

His gaze met hers. He wasn't looking at her as a friend might. The heat in his eyes was unmistakable. "Thanks."

Hope opened her mouth to say 'you're welcome,' only no words came out. She wasn't tongue-tied. He'd rendered her speechless.

Glancing away, she ignored the hammering of her heart and ate her cheeseburger. That didn't stop her from imagining her lips against his. Their softness and sweet taste.

Daydreaming was safe. Anything else with Josh would be… reckless.

They finished eating. The silence between them wasn't awkward, but her body thrummed with awareness of him.

"Having lunch on the beach was a great idea." He rolled up his burger wrapper and napkin and then placed them in the paper bag they'd come in. "Beats being inside."

"I wasn't sure how much beach time you've had since you've been here."

"Not enough, but I'm not leaving for a few more days."

Sunday. That wasn't far away.

He stretched out his legs. He'd traded his flip-flops for a pair of sneakers. Smart move given their sightseeing on foot.

The end of a scar poked out of the bottom of his knee brace. She hadn't noticed that before. The break must have been bad to end his playing career. Yesterday, his limp had been more pronounced in the afternoon when he'd carried in the painting. She hated thinking he was hurting when she was enjoying herself.

"How's your leg holding up?" she asked.

"Good, but sitting is a nice break from all the walking."

"We can stay here as long as you want." Hope placed her hamburger wrapper into the bag. "We're in no rush."

"No one should rush while on vacation."

"I wish my mom had thought like that, but she scheduled our days down to the minute." Hope remembered one trip to Orlando, Florida. Fun, but... "Every trip, we came home exhausted and needing a vacation to recover from the one we took."

"My parents were the opposite. They believed vacations should be all about rest and relaxation." Josh's sunglasses hung off the collar of his T-shirt. The brim from his cap kept the sun off his face. "Our trips weren't the most exciting. We'd visit tourist spots, but we'd also watch movies or play games and spend time together."

"That sounds more my speed." She dug the toe of her sandal in the warm sand. "Though my idea of a vacation is to sit somewhere quiet with my sketchbook and enjoy the view."

He raised his face to the sky, letting the sun kiss his cheeks.

Her breath hitched. Stunning.

His lips curved into a closed-mouthed smile. "I

could get used to this."

He was posed perfectly. Her fingers itched to pull out her notepad and pen and draw him. "You'll have to come back sometime."

"I was thinking the same thing."

Her heart bumped. Anticipation rushed through her.

"Maybe next summer," he continued. "My family would enjoy Indigo Bay."

His family, of course. Hope's shoulders drooped. She blew out a breath.

"Where do you plan to go on vacation next?" he asked.

"No idea. Not counting driving into Charleston, I haven't been anywhere other than Nashville for a couple of years."

Two years and four months. Not that she was counting.

Lines creased his forehead. "Why not?"

She shrugged. That was easier than telling the truth.

His arm went around her. "Hope?"

"The first year I moved back was...hard. I wanted to stay in bed all day. When I felt better, I didn't think about going anywhere. Indigo Bay might not be perfect, but it's..."

"Safe."

"I was going to say home, but yes." Josh's hand was on her shoulder, making her feel warm and tingly all over. She forced herself to sit straight to keep from sinking into him. "I'd like to travel somewhere now. If only so Von would feel more comfortable bringing his girlfriend to the house for a weekend, but I can't take time off from my job at the resort until after Labor Day."

That timing would also allow her to save money for a mini-vacation.

"You should look into places so you're ready when the time comes," Josh encouraged.

Nodding, she tried to reconcile the kind, caring man she'd gotten to know the past three days with the image of an alcoholic who'd been arrested. Tried and failed.

Life could change in an instant—hers had—leaving a person in a sad, dark place. Even if she couldn't picture Josh like that, she'd been there herself. But she'd had Von to help her.

He'd rescued her from New York. Brought her back to Indigo Bay. He'd found her a counselor, driven her to and from the appointments, and built her the studio at his house.

Josh seemed close to his family, but maybe he hadn't had anyone to dedicate themselves to him after his injury. Or maybe the darkness had been too much for him.

Hope wanted to know more about his past, but what happened to him was none of her business. She wouldn't have any words of wisdom for him if she knew the whole story. She knew little about recovery, other than getting sober seemed like a long, difficult process that often took multiple attempts and not everyone succeeded.

Would Josh?

She hoped so.

Kids chased waves only to run away in fits of giggles as the tide rolled in. She longed to feel as carefree and playful as they did.

Someday…

"Ready to continue the tour?" he asked.

Hope stood. "More of Indigo Bay awaits you."

He put his cup into the bag. "Where to next?"

"You're going to need to use your imagination for our next stop."

"That sounds intriguing."

"I want to show, well, tell you about an Indigo Bay Christmas tradition," she explained.

He rose slowly. "Christmas, huh? I'll need to put myself into the right frame of mind for that."

She had no idea what he meant. "Okay."

"Remember what we talked about yesterday? If the timing was right?" He stepped toward her. "You game?"

Her lips parted. She might have nodded.

Josh's mouth touched hers, stealing her breath and maybe her heart.

No, not her heart.

His lips pressed harder against hers until she

thought her knees might give out. Josh backed away with a satisfied expression on his face.

"What was that?" She forced the words out. Difficult to do when her brain was short-circuiting from the way he'd kissed her.

"You told me to use my imagination. That's what I did." He wasn't apologetic at all. "I imagined us standing under mistletoe."

"That's what you meant about the right frame of mind?"

If he'd been a cat, yellow feathers would be sticking out of his pleased smile. "Hey, I can do more than throw a ball. I graduated with a degree in communications. And when the timing is right, my brain just works."

Hope stood there in a daze. "Timing?"

"For another kiss." He winked. "You have to admit it was clever."

"Sly and a tad creative." Hope fought the urge to touch her lips. Heaven help her, but she was ready to step back under the imaginary mistletoe with him. "I'll give you that."

His chest puffed. "Now I'm ready for whatever tradition you want to show me."

Josh left her feeling off-balance. She didn't know if that was him or his kiss or a combination of the two.

"Christmas. Imagination," he offered.

Right. "We need to go to Main Street."

As she headed toward Seaside Boulevard, he fell

into step with her, shortening his strides slightly. She glanced his way to find him staring at her. "What?"

"You're cute when you're flustered," he said.

"I'm not flustered. You caught me off-guard," she clarified. "I'm not used to kisses under imaginary mistletoe."

Or real mistletoe. Or being kissed at all.

"Me, either. But I'll remember that for the future."

With her or someone else? Hope's stomach clenched. She didn't want to know the answer.

"You okay?" Josh asked.

"Fine." Forcing herself to focus, she led him to the most popular spot in town on December twenty-fourth. "At Christmastime, the town places a huge tree right here. It's strung with thousands of lights."

Hope stomped on the spot for emphasis. This Indigo Bay lore was more than Josh needed to know, but she wanted to put in the extra effort if only to remind herself of what they were doing together— sightseeing.

"On the afternoon of Christmas Eve, the town holds a big tree lighting ceremony," she explained in an '*isn't-this-fun*' tone that would make the Chamber of Commerce proud. She could be professional and forget about his kiss. "Before the switch is flipped, residents and visitors line up for a turn to make a wish and place an ornament on the tree."

Josh stared at her as if she'd grown a unicorn horn. "A wish?"

"You wish upon your ornament before hanging it."

"Your town believes in Christmas wishes, yet you teased me about Berry Lake's Bigfoot obsession?" He laughed, a deep, rich sound that drew people's attention. "Let me guess, every store in Indigo Bay sells ornaments for the tree."

"This isn't about commercialism," Hope countered, though he had a point. "Caroline says Christmas wishes are stronger than birthday ones. Some people come every year to hang an ornament."

"And make a wish."

She nodded.

"Your brother is wrong about the West Coast being full of crazies." Amusement lit Josh's eyes. "The South is as weird, but the zany stuff you do is called 'tradition,' so it doesn't seem so far out there."

Hope stared down her nose. "We might be a bit peculiar, but making a Christmas wish is not zany."

"Have any of your wishes come true?" he asked, not flippantly, but the way his eyes searched hers told her he wanted to know.

Thinking back over the years—minus the ones she'd been away in New York—she bit her lip. As a child, her wishes had centered on things, mainly toys. When she was a teenager and in college, her wishes flipped between being a famous painter and finding true love. Now, her wishes had become generic—world peace and a cure for cancer.

"A few have." She remembered two—an American Girl doll and an expensive paint set. "But there's no time limit on wishes."

"What did you wish for?"

"If I tell you, they'll never come true."

"So more than one wish is still out there."

Hope tilted her head, agreeing, though a part of her no longer believed as she once had. Not only in wishes, but in love and happy endings. "No sense wasting a wish on the same thing each year."

"Practical."

That made her laugh. "You're the only person to call an artist practical."

He leaned closer, his shoulder touching hers. "I meant you're practical in making wishes."

"Oh, right."

Except being with Josh had her wishing for some impractical things—more time together and another kiss. She forced a smile.

Ugh. This wasn't good, and she had no idea what to do about it.

11

"I didn't go to a meeting tonight, Rudy." Josh sat on the couch in the cottage. He had his leg elevated on the coffee table using pillows from the spare bedroom. This was his fourth call. He'd already spoken to his family. "I needed to rest my leg."

"On your feet too long?" His sponsor's tone suggested he knew the answer.

"Yes." Jogging this morning had been a bad idea except for seeing Hope for a few minutes. He didn't regret that part. Pain was nothing new, which was why Josh had brought the large ice packs from home. "But sightseeing today was worth it."

Spending time with Hope had been the best part of today. Josh couldn't get enough of her.

Or her kisses.

He'd only gotten one today—a brief one—but that

had been enough.

For now.

She wasn't looking to date. Neither was he. But they could have fun while he was in town. If that included a kiss or two, all the better.

If his leg hadn't been hurting, Josh would have invited Hope to join him for pizza tonight, but he hadn't wanted her to wait on him. From what he'd seen so far, she gave her whole self, whether to her work or to people. He didn't want to take advantage of her kindness. Besides, she would be on her feet all day tomorrow at the wedding. She needed to rest. That was one reason he'd flown her to Nashville yesterday.

"Glad to hear you're enjoying yourself." Rudy sounded like he was smiling. The man had lost his wife and kids due to his drinking, but he hadn't given up on his dream of getting his family back together someday. "You deserve a vacation."

For months, Josh had believed he didn't deserve anything after screwing up so badly. Those closest to him had said he needed to forgive who he used to be and give himself time to figure out who he wanted to be now—the man he was meant to be. They were right, but it still wasn't easy. The more he explored the man he'd been, the more he realized drinking hadn't been his only problem. He hadn't been that good a guy even before his injury and losing himself to the bottle.

Josh had defined himself by being a quarterback. It wasn't what he did for a living, but who he was.

He'd bought into the hype that he was special and deserved more than others. Those he'd thought beneath him hadn't mattered in his mind. Man, he'd been a real jerk.

"I came to Indigo Bay for Jenny," Josh admitted, thinking back to his visit to her house last month. "But this vacation is what I needed. More than I realized."

His trip had turned into a test to see how he did in an unfamiliar place without his usual routine. A reminder he was an adult who could function on his own. A time to relax and have fun.

An image of Hope formed in his mind. Her silky hair falling out of a ponytail. Her lips curved into a soft smile. Her hazel eyes full of affection.

His pulse sprinted, but he wasn't only drawn to how she looked. He'd never met anyone whose mere presence made Josh so… content, as if time could stop and he wouldn't mind because she was with him. He hadn't felt that way before with anyone.

Not even close.

Being around her was a total high. The rush of excitement. The quickening of his pulse.

She made him happy. It was as simple as that.

Josh couldn't wait to see her tomorrow. Maybe he'd call her tonight. Hearing her voice before bedtime would be nice.

"Any other problems besides your leg?" Rudy asked.

"None." Being alone in the cottage was a little

weird, but not in a bad way. "I'm not used to it being so quiet, but I've been meditating and reading. Gives me hope I'll be ready for the new season."

Ready and strong for the travel, hotel rooms, and the temptations of returning to the lifestyle that had made drinking easy to do and hide from his loved ones.

"You're doing great, but don't get too cocky," Rudy said in his typical I'm-older-and-wiser-than-you-kid voice. "You have a wedding to get through on your own. You said beer and wine will be served."

"Yes, but no hard liquor. Jenny said there'll be sparkling apple cider for the toast and other non-alcoholic beverages available." Josh understood Rudy's concern, and he'd brought up the reception when he was at the meeting last night. "The reception would be easier if Sam were with me, but I've had dinner with others who were drinking. This shouldn't be that different."

"You'll have to wait and see about that." Rudy paused. Something he often did when he was mulling over what to say next. "What's your plan for the reception?"

Josh had figured this out over a week ago. "I'll make a point to say something to the bartender when I arrive. I have you or Sam to call if I need to talk to someone. The reception is at the same place I'm staying. I can walk to my cottage if I need to get away."

"Sounds good," Rudy said. "Keep a non-alcoholic

drink in hand at the reception. That'll avoid the likelihood of someone offering you a drink you don't want."

"I'll do that." Josh's confidence brimmed. He liked the feeling. "I know this might be harder than I think because I've limited myself to where I go or what I do since rehab, but I have a good feeling about tomorrow."

He would not ruin Jenny's wedding day. Nor would he bother her. If he needed someone to talk to in person, he didn't think Hope would mind.

"You've limited those things because you know yourself. Recovery is a long road. You're almost eleven months in. You're doing well, but relapses can happen to the best of us. You know my story. That's why you need to stay vigilant."

"I'm trying to do that." Josh hoped he sounded as strong as he felt.

A knock sounded on the front door.

"Someone's here, Rudy." Josh carefully stood, allowed his leg a moment to adjust after being elevated. "I'll call you tomorrow."

"I'm here whenever. Take care." With that, the line disconnected.

Josh hobbled to the door. He opened it. "Jenny."

"Hi." Standing next to her was a tall man with short hair. Both wore shorts, T-shirts, and flip-flops. "This is my fiancé, Dare O'Rourke."

Dare extended his arm and shook Josh's hand.

"Thanks for flying Jenny's dress and the other items to Indigo Bay."

"Happy to help." Josh stared at the two. He remembered Dare was five years younger than Jenny, but he couldn't see that much difference in their ages, especially with the loving way the groom stared at his bride-to-be.

As Jenny's eyes widened, she scrunched her nose. "What's wrong with your leg?"

"It's a little sore after sightseeing." He'd been trying to keep his weight off it, using the door for support. "I'll be fine."

"Dude, I recognize those ice packs. My physical therapist called them the big guns." Dare's face tightened. He grabbed Jenny's hand, pulling her inside the cottage. "What are you doing standing up? Get off your feet now."

Before Josh could say anything, Dare wrapped his arm around him to keep weight off his leg. The guy was an inch shorter but solid muscle. Not surprising given he was an Army Ranger. "Hop to the couch."

Jenny closed the door. "Have you eaten?"

"Yes," Josh said, grateful to sit and prop his leg again. "I have leftovers if you're hungry."

She went into the kitchen. The refrigerator door opened.

He parted his lips to say something, but Dare shushed him.

"Nothing you say will stop her from doing

whatever it is she wants to do," Dare said.

"Speaking from experience?"

Nodding, he grinned wryly. "For someone so quiet, she can be mule stubborn."

"I heard that," Jenny called out from the kitchen.

"I love you," Dare yelled, his blue eyes full of amusement. He winked at Josh. "Those three words are pure magic."

Josh laughed. Maybe someday he'd get to try that magic out for himself.

She returned with a glass of ginger ale and two cookies on a paper towel. "I would have made tea, but it's a little warm for that."

"This works." Josh took the glass and sipped. "What brings you by the night before your wedding?"

Jenny glanced at Dare, who gave her an encouraging look before reaching out to hold her hand.

"Missy is my matron of honor. Tara, a friend from my online book club who lives in Savannah, will be there with her husband, Heath. Everyone else attending is either an acquaintance or here for Dare, except you." Jenny took a breath. "During the ceremony, the bride's family sits in the front row on the left. Flowers will be on the first three seats as a memorial to my parents and brother, but I would like you to sit in that row, too. If you wouldn't mind."

The air rushed from Josh's lungs. A band seemed to tighten around his chest. Her request touched him at a gut level.

"I'd be honored," he said, having to force the words out. "Thank you."

Josh wanted to say more, but Jenny's request overwhelmed him. Maybe there was hope for him.

Dare kissed the top of Jenny's hand. "What did I tell you?"

She shrugged. "I don't like to assume anything."

"Says the woman who flies to Texas because a man she never met in real life asks her to come while he's drifting in and out of consciousness," Dare joked, alluding to how he'd met his future wife after knowing her online. "And I'm glad you did that, babe, or we wouldn't be here today."

Jenny sighed. "It was meant to be."

"Fate," Josh said.

Staring at each other, Jenny and Dare nodded. Love poured between the two.

Emotion tightened Josh's throat. He wanted to reach out and grab a handful of that love for himself.

I want that.

Just as he had in Nashville when he saw Cami and Dan together.

Would he ever find the kind of love Jenny and Dare shared?

His relationships, if he wanted to call them that, had been brief, some only one night. The women had been another crutch, one he'd used longer than alcohol. The casual dating and hook-up mentality wouldn't satisfy him now. He wanted…

Josh thought of Hope. As her image filled the void inside him, a smile spread across his face. She was giving him hope that if he remained sober, maybe he could have the things he'd once dreamed about. Not the illustrious football career but a wife and kids.

A family of his own.

That was possible for him, wasn't it?

* * *

Hope had finished washing the dishes, but she wasn't ready for bed. Settling on the couch, she turned on the television. The show, a hospital-based drama, was easy to ignore when all she wanted to do was go over her day with Josh.

She'd had fun, but her feelings for him left her confused. Being friends with someone shouldn't have her mixed-up and questioning every word and action. Granted, she wasn't used to kissing friends. Maybe it wasn't Josh per se, but his kisses that muddled her brain.

Though today's peck had been just a playful brush of lips. A joke.

Except the tingles had lasted for… hours.

The more she told herself the kiss was no big deal, the more she realized it had been. For her at least.

A text notification sounded. She glanced at her phone.

Josh: *Are you still awake?*
Hope: *Yes.*

Her phone rang. She didn't need to look at the screen to know who it was. "How's your leg?"

Silence filled the line. "Why are you asking about my leg?"

"You favored it more as the day went on."

"Oh." The one word spoke volumes, and she fought the urge to ask if she could come over to help him. "I've been icing and elevating it," he added.

She straightened with a sense of urgency. "Is it better?"

"Getting there."

She knew from her brother that was about as much as she'd get out of Josh. Men never liked admitting weaknesses. "Stay off it in the morning."

"No jogging." He sounded amused. "My mom and sister laid down the law earlier."

"They care." *So do I.*

More than Hope realized, and she didn't know what that meant.

Her temples throbbed.

"I had a great time today," he said.

"Me, too, but I'm sorry you're in pain."

"It's not that bad. Honest." He sounded sincere. "But what little hurt I'm feeling… totally worth it."

"Thanks, I think." Still, a smile tugged on her lips.

"It's true." His voice was firmer. "The real reason

I'm resting my leg tonight is so I can show off my moves on the dance floor."

"Sounds like another injury waiting to happen," she joked.

"Or *Dancing with the Stars* might call."

"You think?"

"If they get desperate."

She laughed. "I can't wait. To see you, I mean. Dance." She nearly groaned. Maybe she should shut up now.

"I feel the same way about seeing you." He yawned. "'cuse me."

He sounded like a little boy trying to talk as he kept yawning. "Time for bed."

"Is this where we switch to Skype and show each other what we're wearing?" he joked.

He was teasing her. That was what friends did. Not, um, Skype like... *that*. "Haha. I'm hanging up now."

His soft laugh covered her like a fleece blanket— soft and warm and just right. "See you tomorrow."

Hope couldn't wait.

* * *

On Friday afternoon as Zoe double-checked the setup on the beach for the ceremony, Hope finished setting the tables for the reception. She glanced over to where Paula was arranging the three-tiered wedding cake she'd made for Jenny and Dare's reception.

Seashells cascaded down one side of the cake. The white-on-white color scheme was both bridal and stunning. The topper wasn't the traditional bride and groom figurines, but a message in a bottle.

Hope moved closer to her friend, who was adjusting one of her plastic gloves and trying not to get frosting on herself. "That is your best yet."

Paula wore her black hair in a bun. "I'm happy with how this one turned out. It took a few tries to get the seashells right, but they came out nicely."

"They're perfect." Hope stared at the decorations with longing for what she'd never experienced. Marrying Adam at city hall had meant no flowers, no white dress, no wedding cake. Instead, they'd gone out to a nice dinner with two of his friends who'd been witnesses. There hadn't been time for her family to get to New York to attend. "The cake looks… fabulous."

Paula stared at her creation with pride. "Thanks."

Hope read the piece of paper inside the bottle. "Jenny and Dare. A couple brought together by the sea. A love meant to be." Her hand touched her chest. "That is so sweet."

"I loved that they wanted a topper that was meaningful to them as a couple." Her smile widened. "They hadn't said anything specific about the message, so I wrote something for them."

"They'll love it." Hope stared at her petite friend who had never looked happier. "Your cakes are in high demand. You're in a great relationship. What's your secret?"

"I wish I knew, but I just never gave up even when I wasn't sure things would work out." Mischief glinted in Paula's blue-gray eyes. "Is that handsome ex-football player turned sportscaster the reason for your question?"

"What? No." Hope didn't know what to say, especially after their phone call last night. Her thoughts had kept her awake for hours after they'd hung up. "We're friends."

Paula's mouth quirked. "Friends who've seen each other every day he's been in town."

"Okay, I'll admit he's easy on the eyes. Any woman with a pulse would agree he's handsome regardless if they are in a relationship."

"Yes, but we're not talking about other women." Paula added more seashells around the bottom of the cake. "We're talking about you."

"I like him." Hope tried to sound casual.

Paula gave her a look. "Like or *like*?"

"He's a nice guy. We have fun together."

"It's about time you had fun." Paula adjusted a starfish on the cake. "I knew you couldn't put off dating forever."

Hope sighed. "We're not…"

"Spending time together? Kissing?" Paula raised her dark eyebrows that contrasted sharply against her pale, lightly freckled skin. "Because that looked like a

152

hot kiss you shared on the deck the other day."

Heat burned Hope's face. She hadn't thought anyone would see that. But then again, Paula lived next door and had a view of the deck from her kitchen. "It was."

"And?"

Hope shrugged. "I'll see him at the wedding, but he's leaving Sunday. There's nothing more to say."

Unfortunately.

"Really?" Paula sighed. "Technology makes long-distance relationships easier."

Hope grimaced. "It's too soon to talk about something like that. We hardly know each other."

"Quality over quantity."

Okay, their times together had been good. No, great. She couldn't stop thinking about him or wanting to be with him, but still… "It's too soon."

"That's Von talking. Not you."

"You're not going to give up, are you?"

"Nope, because I don't want what happened with your ex to make you turn away from a better man in the future," Paula admitted. "I don't know if this new guy is the one, but you haven't made any new friends since I met you. You sure haven't kissed anyone since Adam. Something about Josh is different. You should figure out what that is."

This was why Hope loved having Paula as a friend—like Von, she never held back, even if she might be misguided here. "Did you miss the part that

Josh is leaving on Sunday?"

"That gives you the rest of today since he'll be at the wedding, and all of tomorrow." Paula had an answer for everything. "Plenty of time to get to know him better."

"But why?" Hope's self-preservation mode wasn't kicking in like it usually did, but that watch-yourself feeling was still there. "I don't want a relationship."

"You didn't want one," Paula clarified in that patient tone of hers. "Who's to say you'll always feel that way?"

Josh made Hope feel warm and tingly inside. Talking to him over the phone last night had left her feeling as giddy as a teenager. But Hope wasn't about to admit that to anyone. Or that she'd dreamt about him for the past two nights. Or that she was trying not to get attached to him, but feared it might be too late.

She swallowed. "I have no idea how I'll feel someday, but I don't want my heart broken again."

A glance at the tables told her the centerpieces needed to be put out. She'd light the candles after the ceremony.

"I need to get back to work." Hope took a step away from the cake and Paula.

"Don't let fear stop you from pursuing something that might be good for you, okay?"

"I won't." Truth was, Hope wasn't ready to say goodbye to Josh. She didn't know what that meant or where that left her. Them?

Not that there was a them.

She glanced at the bottle on the top of the wedding cake.

A couple meant to be.

Hope wished she knew how Josh felt about her. Maybe that would help her figure out how she felt about him.

12

Josh arrived at the beach early. Talking to Hope last night, hearing her voice before he fell asleep, had given him the best night of sleep in days. Maybe weeks. He'd woken up rested and thinking about her. He was excited for Jenny's wedding, but he couldn't wait to see Hope again.

And there she was.

As his gaze took her in, he froze, even his heartbeat seemed to still. She wore an above-the-knee pink dress that showed off her honey-gold skin. Her hair was pulled back in a loose braid with tendrils framing her face.

Josh forced his feet to move across the sand toward her.

She stood at the back of the four rows of white chairs tied with big bows, separated by an aisle that led to an arched trellis covered in tulle and seashells. All the seats were empty, but she hadn't noticed him yet. She was busy straightening a bow on the last row of chairs.

"Hey." He stopped three feet away. Any closer and he might reach out to touch her. Yeah, she was that beautiful. "Your dress is great."

"Work clothes." With a grin, she gave him a once over. "You clean up nicely yourself. Linen suit?"

Josh nodded. He'd purchased the tan suit for an event last year that he couldn't remember, but he'd found an empty flask in the jacket pocket and tossed it in the garbage.

"Ready for the big day?" he asked.

"As ready as we ever are." She glanced over at the setup for the ceremony. "The breeze will help keep guests cool, but it's not strong enough to do any damage to the trellis or the bride's hair."

He liked how the wind toyed with Hope's hair. "Everything looks great."

Especially her.

"That's all Zoe's doing and why she's in charge of guest services and events." The wind moved several papers on a nearby linen-covered table that held a guestbook, feathered pen, and a matted photo of the bride and groom. Hope placed a large seashell on the papers. "I'm her worker bee."

Hope could buzz around him anytime. He stepped closer.

She handed him a pen. "Sign the guestbook and the photo's mat."

He did, then set the pen on the table. "Can I see you later?"

"I'll be working at the reception."

"After that." He wanted to make sure she understood what he meant. Their phone call last night had been good, but that wasn't what he wanted tonight. Not when he was leaving in two days. "Just you and me."

"Oh." She dragged her teeth over her lower lip. She didn't appear hesitant, more contemplative. "Um, sure. I have to clean up the multipurpose room after everyone leaves, but I can text you when I'm finished."

"Sounds good." The words came out quickly, as if he needed to say them before she changed her mind. Not that she seemed like she would, but something about Hope flustered him. "I'll wait for you outside the multipurpose room."

Guests walked toward them. Hope picked up papers from beneath the shell and gave him one. "Here's the program."

He went to the front row. The first three seats on his left contained small bouquets with white and purple flowers and a nametag—Mom, Dad, Rob. Josh had only seen Mr. and Mrs. Hanford at school events and around town, but he'd met Rob, who was a few years younger than him. Rob had been a wrestler. Nice guy, spent all his spare time with his then-girlfriend, Missy, according to Sam, who'd known him better and made fun of Rob for being crazy in love with his girlfriend.

Josh sat in the fourth seat. He angled himself to see the other rows of chairs behind him. As other guests arrived, he took pictures for his mom and Ava. Both would want a full report of the wedding. He snapped photos of Hope as she passed out programs and handed off the pen.

Her wide smile shouted out to the world how much she loved her job working events. She seemed so at ease, and her face glowed.

He couldn't stop staring.

A young Hispanic man arrived in a wheelchair being carried by four guys in suits and military haircuts. Another man, a few years older than the others and wearing his dress uniform, followed them.

Josh couldn't hear what Hope said to the men, but she led them to a special spot where they placed the wheelchair.

The man in uniform spoke to the others, and they laughed. "That's why I'm the staff sergeant and in charge of you clowns."

"Clowns, huh?" The man in the wheelchair grinned. "Guess trying to have a kid is making you rethink the language you use, sir."

The man in uniformed shrugged. "Lizzy figures if I start now, then by the time we get around to having a baby, I'll no longer swear."

Another man snickered. "Good luck with that,

Hamilton."

More laughter sounded. They must be part of Dare's Ranger platoon.

A few minutes later, a woman with dark hair and three young women who resembled her took the front row on the opposite side of the aisle. That must be Dare's mom and his three younger sisters.

Music played from a violin and cellist. At the altar, Dare and his best man, Staff Sergeant Mitchell Hamilton according to the wedding program, both in dress uniform, stood with the officiant, a woman in her forties with a ready smile and kind eyes.

Missy strolled down the aisle in a lavender dress that flowed around her knees. Her bouquet contained the same flowers as the ones on the seats next to him. Her eyes gleamed as if she were ready to cry, but the smile showed her happiness for her sister-in-law.

Next came Jenny, who had never smiled so brightly.

Dare stared as if captivated by his bride.

Josh didn't blame the groom. He hadn't seen what was inside the dress bag he'd delivered to the dry cleaners, but the gown was perfect on her. Lace with a high-neck bodice, short sleeves, and a big bow in the back. No veil. She wore her hair up with white and purple flowers artfully positioned. He fought the urge to glance over his shoulder to see what Hope was doing. Instead, he forced himself to face forward and listen to the words being said.

As Jenny and Dare exchanged vows, Josh wiped his eyes. Sand, he told himself. Though the words of love and devotion from the bride and groom left him choked up.

"I now pronounce you husband and wife," the officiant said. "You may kiss the bride."

Dare leaned forward. Jenny met him halfway to press her lips against his.

The military guys whistled, cheered, and high fived. Their staff sergeant shook his head.

The wedding party marched up the aisle to applause. As the photographer went off with the newlyweds to take pictures, Zoe directed the guests toward the reception site.

Where was Hope? At the reception already?

Josh headed that way. He wondered what she thought of the wedding. Granted, this was her job, but she seemed like the kind of person who would take an interest in her clients.

Inside the multipurpose room, he stared in disbelief. It didn't look at all as it had on Tuesday.

"Do you like the decorations?" Hope asked from behind him.

He faced her. "I'm stunned at the transformation."

Tulle, seashells, flowers, and small white lights topped the panels on each of the four walls, but that was only the beginning. More tulle and lights hung from various edges of the room, strung to the center where a lighting fixture hung. The effect reminded

Josh of a starfish. A round table held the wedding cake. Four other tables of eight had been set up in the room. Each table had a beach-themed centerpiece containing sand, seashells, candles, and a message in a bottle. A bar was in one corner, a DJ in the other.

"I hope the bride and groom will be pleased," she said.

"They'll be ecstatic."

"You can get something to drink and then find your table." She motioned to a board with the table numbers on it. "I need to talk to the caterer."

Josh wished she was his plus-one tonight instead of working the event. "Go. We'll have time together later."

* * *

The bride and groom glowed with love for each other, wedding guests smiled as they ate and drank, and Hope's feet only ached a little after being on them for hours. She'd call that a win.

Being in the same space with Josh for a few hours, even if she couldn't talk to him while she was working, was the icing, even tastier than Paula's amazing cake creation. Hope had tasted a small piece that had been mangled during the cutting.

Delicious.

Josh danced with one of Dare's sisters—Kate, or maybe that was Fiona. His wide smile deepened the lines at the corners of his eyes. Seeing him having fun pleased Hope. He'd had an endless supply of partners tonight, including the bride and Lizzy Hamilton, the wife of the best man, who'd glowered at Josh while they'd danced.

Not that Hope was paying that close attention. Or jealous.

Okay, maybe a little.

But she was working. What Josh did shouldn't matter. At least she wished it didn't.

Zoe handed Hope a water bottle. "Things are winding down, but you've got cleanup ahead of you. Take a fifteen-minute break."

The first time Hope had worked an event for Zoe, she'd turned down the opportunity for a break. She'd ended up with sore muscles and a blister. That was the last time she'd said no.

"Thanks."

Without wanting to waste a single minute, she headed out of the double doors, cut through the patio, and plopped onto one of the lounge chairs on the sand. The air was warmer outside. It was quieter, too. No pounding bass line, no taps against crystal wanting the bride and groom to kiss, nothing to do but relax for a few minutes. She'd take off her shoes to give her swollen feet a break if she thought she could get them on again. Better not chance it.

A few sips of water and resting for a few would give her a second wind. Something she'd need for cleanup detail.

"Taking a break?"

Josh.

Chills shot down her arms. She hadn't expected to see him out here.

Straightening, she turned toward him. Her mouth went dry.

He carried a favor bucket and his jacket. The sleeves of his white button-up were rolled up. The casual look suited him.

Hope raised her water bottle. "My boss took pity on me.

"You've been working hard."

"You've been dancing nonstop." She patted the spot next to her. "How's the leg?"

"Holding up." He sat, his thigh pressing against hers. Heat emanated at the point of contact, even though clothing separated their skin. "It's a friendly crowd."

"Dare's single guy friends seem more interested in drinking."

"That makes me one of the only sober partner choices tonight." He placed his jacket and bucket on the end of the lounge chair. "Though I'd rather be dancing with you."

Her heart stumbled. "I'd like that, too, if I wasn't working."

He glanced around. "You aren't right now."

"No, but…"

Josh pulled her out of view from the multipurpose room, took out his cell phone from his pant pocket, and tapped the screen. A romantic ballad played.

The song was unexpected. "Ed Sheeran is on your playlist?"

"My sister loves this song." Josh tried to sound nonchalant. He almost pulled it off.

Hope bit back a laugh. "You're a good brother."

The setting sun splashed the sky in an artistic blend of oranges, lavenders, pinks, and yellows. The colorful combination couldn't hide the pink on Josh's cheeks. How someone could be both gorgeous and adorable at the same time was beyond her, but he was.

His gaze met hers. An electrical current seemed to run between them, connecting them in a tangible way.

Her breath caught. She didn't know what would happen next, but she couldn't wait to find out.

Josh held out his hand. "May I have this dance?"

She clasped her fingers with his. "I'd be honored."

As the music played, he pulled her into his arms and swayed. He rubbed her back. Each touch made her heart melt. The sand wasn't the best dancing surface, especially with wobbly knees. Those had nothing to do with being on her feet all day, and everything to do with her dance partner. But she wouldn't change this moment for anything.

"I've been trying to figure out a way to dance with you," he said.

"You succeeded." Hope nearly laughed because

what she felt for Josh went so far beyond friendship she wasn't sure how to define it. For some reason, that didn't freak her out. She was tired of holding back the way she had for the past two years. If anything, Josh made her want to step out of her box… to take a chance.

The desire flowing through her veins matched the heat in his eyes. That was the only invitation she needed because the timing was… right. Only it was her turn to grab the kiss she wanted.

She rose on her tiptoes. Pressed her lips against his. Hard.

Forget gentle and soft. This kiss was full of longing. She hadn't wanted to admit her growing affection for him, but she couldn't ignore it now with their tongues tangling.

He tasted sweet with a hint of chocolate. The apple cider and the cake? She didn't care. It was the perfect combination.

As Josh's arms tightened around her, she arched against him. With each touch of his lips, her fears faded. His embrace brought a sense of belonging and acceptance, two things she hadn't known she needed but now wasn't sure she could do without.

"Hope," Zoe called across the courtyard.

She pulled back. Were her lips as red and swollen as his? Probably given the way they throbbed. "That's my boss. I have to go back to work."

He lowered his arms. "Thanks for the dance

and…"

"You're welcome." Except she would rather be in his embrace again. "Are we still on for later?"

"Definitely." He ran his finger along her jaw. "Text me, and I'll be here."

"Are you heading back into the reception?" she asked.

"It's getting a little too rowdy," he admitted. "I've said my goodbyes to the bride and the groom. I'm going to drop off the favor bucket and my jacket at the cottage and then take a walk."

She picked up her water bottle from next to the lounge chair.

He laughed. "You are a worker bee."

"Buzz." She touched the tip of his nose. "Be careful, or you might get stung."

He winked. "I'll take my chances."

Would she? For the first time in a long time, she was ready.

Her heart hammered against her rib cage. She couldn't wait for the reception to be over. "See you soon."

13

A little while later, Josh was on Main Street. His plan to survive the reception had worked. If he wasn't dancing, he'd held a glass of mineral water or a flute of sparkling cider. The bartender, who'd dealt with guests like him before, had his refills ready for him. Josh had left as the beer chugging got underway.

Thinking how he'd handled the evening sent a rush of pride through him. He'd remained in control. Focused. Happy.

Being sober hadn't affected his fun. If anything, he'd had a better time than the last wedding where he couldn't even recall the bride or groom's names. Josh would remember Jenny and Dare's ceremony, the reception, and his brief interlude with...

Hope.

The heels of his dress shoes clapped against the

sidewalk. He focused on the sound to keep himself in the moment because all he wanted to do was float away in his memory of kissing Hope.

She'd kissed him.

Her making the first move had been both a thrill and a turn-on. He couldn't wait to find out what the rest of tonight held because his lips still tingled from her kisses.

Soon.

He doubted he'd hear from Hope for another hour. That would give him time to settle his anxious nerves. Not that he had any reason to be nervous. His past didn't seem to bother Hope, and he'd succeeded at the reception.

Was that enough? Was he?

Josh wished he knew.

No matter how well he'd done tonight, or any day since his arrest, the past hung over him like a dark cloud about to unleash a torrential thunderstorm and drown him once again. He couldn't quite shake what he'd done or the man he'd been. The bottle had controlled him for so long—imaging a future where he made the decisions still seemed like a pipe dream.

Or had.

Until meeting Hope.

She made him want to focus on the future and put the past behind him once and for all.

But could he do that?

Josh glanced at his cell phone in case he'd missed

hearing a text notification. Nothing from Hope, but his brother and sister both wanted to know how things were going.

He went into the Chocolate Emporium where he ordered a peanut cluster and a soda before sitting to rest his leg and text his family. A few people inside gave him second and third glances, but thankfully no one approached him. Good, because he'd forgotten to wear a baseball cap. That wouldn't go with his suit.

Keeping his head down to avoid making eye contact with anyone, he downed his drink before throwing his trash away and leaving the chocolate shop.

A few people milled about, but not as many as were out during the afternoons. He'd make his way back toward the resort. By the time he got there, maybe Hope would be finished.

Music poured out of the open door of a bar. Funny, but he hadn't realized this place existed.

"Josh, right?" A young woman stood in the bar's doorway. "You're Jenny's friend."

He nodded.

"I'm Claire, one of Dare's sisters." She glanced over her shoulder and then back at him. She frowned. "Two of his friends are here and have had way too much to drink. They're ready to pass out or start a fight. I'd rather not disturb Dare on his wedding night, and I don't have Mitch Hamilton's number. Could you please help me get them back to their cottage?"

Josh had made it through the reception, but going into a bar…

A shiver ran down his spine. Goose bumps pricked his skin. Claire had no idea what she was asking. He hadn't been in a bar in almost a year. But he couldn't leave her to deal with this herself. That wouldn't be right when he'd been so intoxicated at times he'd needed others to step up to get him home safely.

"Sure," he said.

"Thanks." The tension in her face lessened, but her posture remained stiff. "I should have never offered to be their DW."

"DW?"

"Designated walker. A driver isn't required since we're staying so close to Main Street." She sighed. "This serves me right for thinking one of them was cute. Dare tried to warn me, but I thought he was going all big brother on me."

Josh wouldn't want Ava to have to deal with drunks, and she was at least a decade older than Claire. "We'll get them back to the cottage."

"Thanks."

Staring at the bar's entrance, he squared his shoulders.

I've got this.

Just like the reception.

Josh took a breath before forcing himself to go inside. The sights and sounds hit him like a punch to the solar plexus. The smells overwhelmed and intoxicated him.

Home.

Being inside was like coming home. People might not know his name here, but the atmosphere of kinship and alcohol-fueled acceptance was the same as any other place he'd frequented.

Claire motioned for him to follow. "They're by the bar."

Two men Josh recognized from the wedding sat on stools downing shots. One slammed his glass against the bar. "Another round."

Claire grimaced. "The shots are after the beer and wine at the reception."

He could barely hear her over the music and the hooting and shouting crowd. Patrons slurred their words as they ordered more drinks from the tray-carrying waitresses in shorts and tight T-shirts.

Get out.

Except he couldn't. Not until he helped Claire.

Behind the bar, the bottles sitting on shelves glowed and called to him as if they contained the answer to every problem in the world. Once they had, or so he'd believed. Now…

Someone backed into him. "Sorry, bro."

"No problem," Josh said automatically.

"Well, I'll be." The man's breath smelled like beer from a keg that had been sitting out in the sun too long. He slapped Josh on the shoulder. "Miss seeing you on the field each Sunday, number eighteen."

"Thanks." Josh tried to get closer to Claire, but the guy blocked his way.

"Have one on me." The guy shoved a shot glass of tequila in Josh's hand, some of the amber liquid sloshing onto his skin. "That's the least I can do after the money you won me with my Fantasy Football team."

Transfixed, Josh stared at the drink. His fingers tightened painfully around the glass, his brain unsure if it were a magic elixir or deadly poison. Thoughts crashed through him, but one was louder than the rest.

Think how much easier it will be to deal with the two drunks at the bar with some liquid courage. One drink will settle you down. That way you'll be relaxed and ready to see Hope.

He knew that inner voice—had listened and done what it said so many times.

You've still got it, Cooper. Come on. It's only one drink. You can handle a little shot.

* * *

Standing in the courtyard, Hope glanced at her cell. No reply from Josh yet. The multipurpose room was cleaned and locked. She'd sent the first text to him over thirty minutes ago.

Where was he?

She shook her phone as if that would make a

difference. Still no reply.

What was going on?

He'd said he would meet her here. She'd confirmed their plans after their dance.

After the kiss.

Had something happened or had he changed his mind?

Thoughts tangled together, but one screamed louder than the rest.

He's not coming.

Hope didn't know whether to laugh or cry. She'd finally taken a chance and gone after what she wanted… only to be stood up.

Karma? Fate? Whichever it was, it had to be laughing at her.

Trying had to count for something, right? Paula would be happy Hope hadn't given up, and Von…

Her brother would say "I told you so" if she told him what happened. A good thing he was staying at his place in Charleston this weekend. Probably better if she told no one about this.

The silent phone mocked her as much as her thoughts. Hope's shoulders slumped, feeling as if bags of sand had been piled on top of them.

Josh doesn't care about you.

You were someone convenient to spend time with.

He's with another woman.

What was she doing? Thinking? She had no idea what was going on. Why think the worst?

Maybe his leg was hurting, and he'd stayed at his cottage. Maybe he'd fallen asleep. Maybe he'd gone to a late-night support meeting. They had those, right?

One excuse followed another. She wasn't named Hope for nothing. Except…

A sour taste coated her mouth. She wrapped her arms around her knot-filled stomach.

When Adam's lover had confessed their affair, Hope had spent the rest of the day making similar excuses for her husband. Anything to believe she hadn't been betrayed and lied to by the man she loved. She'd almost been able to convince herself they weren't over until he'd blamed her for his cheating. That was when she knew the marriage was over.

And she'd lost it.

Hope wasn't about to borrow worry, but she wouldn't justify being blown off by Josh, either. She typed out another text—her third, but who was counting other than her?

Hope: *Haven't heard from you, so I'm going home.*

Short and sweet.

No asking if he'd danced too much and his leg was hurting. No asking if he was tired and needed to sleep. No asking if he wanted her to be there and help him.

Not her job.

Send the message. If he'd wanted to see you tonight, he would have replied. He would be here.

Hope hit send.

The message showed delivered, but no reply came. With a sigh, she removed her shoes from her sore feet and put on flip-flops instead.

Time to go home.

Though she doubted she'd be able to sleep.

* * *

Josh stood at Hope's door, feeling like an idiot and a loser. Of course, he was both. She deserved better, but he had no place else to go.

He rang the doorbell.

He'd thought he was getting better, stronger, but the temptation was still there. And always would be.

He'd hadn't truly grasped that.

Until tonight.

Where was Hope? He'd seen her texts. She said she would be home.

He hit the doorbell again.

Josh had been told many times that once an alcoholic, always an alcoholic. He'd never believed it, even if he said the words. But he realized tonight he would always be an alcoholic.

Fear flowed through him. Fear of failing himself and those who cared about him.

Maybe the doorbell was broken.

176

He knocked. The frenetic sound echoed the beat of his heart.

"Who is it?" Hope asked through the closed door.

"Josh." His voice sounded strangled.

The door flew open. Her hurt-filled eyes widened. She wore a pair of shorts and an oversized T-shirt. Her fingers gripped the doorknob. "I texted you and waited a half hour."

"I'm sorry." He imagined what she saw in that instant because he felt as if he'd taken ten steps back tonight. He must look a mess.

Who was he kidding? He was a mess.

This is who you are.

Who you might always be.

No, he didn't want to settle for that. Josh wanted to be more than a drunk wanting his next drink. If not, he would have stayed at the bar. He wouldn't have called Rudy. He wouldn't be here. "I'm so, so sorry."

Josh didn't know what else to say.

Questions filled her gaze, but something else, too. Compassion. She opened the door wider. "Come inside."

He released the breath he'd been holding. His steps hesitant, he crossed the threshold slowly, his usual confidence overrun by doubt and uncertainty.

"Sit." She motioned to the couch. "Did something happen?"

Unable to answer, Josh sat. His hands trembled, and he clasped them together. He focused on his breathing—a trick he'd learned during rehab.

She touched his arm. "Can I get you anything?"

His throat was Sahara dry. "Water, please."

"I'll be right back." Hope went into the kitchen. Ice cubes dropped into a glass.

He'd been so careful up to this point in his recovery. Sure, he'd been around others who drank. He'd passed through the wine section at grocery stores. He'd made it through the reception. He thought he had a better handle on his sobriety.

But he hadn't.

Not even close if he went by tonight.

She returned with two glasses of water, placed them on the coffee table, and sat next to him. At least she wasn't keeping her distance. "If you want something to eat, let me know."

"Thanks." He sipped his water. Thirsty or procrastinating, he wasn't sure. "I'm sorry for barging in on you so late. I was on the phone with Rudy, my sponsor, when you were texting. He'd still be on the phone with me, but I wanted to talk to someone in person. I had nowhere else to go but here. Well, except back to the bar."

Hope stiffened. "The bar?"

"I didn't drink, but I wanted to. Oh, how I wanted to." Josh scrubbed his hands over his face, wishing he could wipe away what happened. He'd tried to be the man he wanted to be—a decent man, not a drunk. "I was so tempted I feel like I failed."

"You can't help how you feel, but the fact you're here and not at the bar means you won." She held his hand. "How did you end up there in the first place?"

"I was over on Main Street waiting to hear from you." He clung to Hope like a lifeline. "One of Dare's sisters saw me. She asked if I'd help her get two of Dare's friends, who'd drunk too much, back to their cottage."

"So you went in there to help—not to drink." It wasn't a question, but the relief in Hope's voice was clear.

"Drinking was the last thing on my mind," he admitted. "But as soon as I entered…"

The memory of the smells assaulted him.

"It was like coming home after being away for far too long. I felt as if I belonged. Someone recognized me. Handed me a shot. I held the glass. Smelled the tequila. The adrenaline rush was strong. I'd missed that. More than I realized."

"Is this your first time feeling that way?"

"No, but it's been a while. I've avoided putting myself in situations like this." He shook his head. "A little voice said '*it's only one drink*'. Even though I knew it would matter, and I'd never stop with one drink, I held onto that shot glass like it was as necessary to my survival as oxygen. Worse, I was so caught up in myself that Dare's sister was on her own with the drunks. I was selfish when I should have been selfless. If one of Dare's friends hadn't fallen off his stool, I might have downed that shot."

Josh squeezed his eyes shut, but that didn't stop the scene from playing in his mind as if on an endless loop. "I've been going to meetings and doing what I'm supposed to do. I thought I was further along in my recovery. I thought I would be different from everyone else. I believed I'd kick this and not be tempted again. But I'm the same as everyone else who has gone through this. Each day is getting better, but it's still a battle. One I feel I'm losing now."

He cradled his head in his hands.

"Hey." She wrapped her arm around him. Pulled him closer. "Tonight was hard on you. I get that, but it'll be okay."

Hearing her words made him want to believe them.

Being with her was what he needed. The sweet scent of her filled his senses. The tension seeped from his body. He relaxed into her.

"I gave back the drink without taking a sip. We got the two guys to their cottage and left them in the care of one of their friends who wasn't drunk. As soon as I left, I called Rudy. He talked me off the edge. I headed toward your house. He didn't want to hang up, but I told him I had a place to go, someone to be with who would listen and help me. You."

Hope hugged him. "You did the right thing by not drinking or going back to the bar after you'd left. You called for support and came here."

"I'm a wreck." The words came out rough and raw as if his heart had been ripped from his chest.

"That's okay. Staying sober can't be easy, but you're doing it." She let go of him and straightened. "I'm proud of you for coming here, for trusting me to help rather than turning to the bottle. I respect you so much."

He wanted to scream stop. She was being too nice to him.

Josh lowered his gaze to his dress shoes. "I haven't done anything to earn your pride or respect."

His words were hushed. His strength and hope gone, defeated by the knowledge he might not have slipped up tonight, but he would…eventually.

"Don't say that." Her tone was harsh, not what he expected. "The first step to overcoming a problem is admitting you have one. That's what you did. Do you know how many people can't do that or even realize there's an issue? I don't know what you're going through, but you've been sober since July, right? That's a big deal. And you're being way too hard on yourself. Don't discount what you've been doing or how far you've come."

"I'll try not to." Hope was incredible. She grounded him. Made him want to succeed. But she deserved better than him. "Thank you."

"You're welcome." Her closed-mouthed smile spread. "I want to help you, Josh. Whatever you need. Just ask or tell me."

His heart pounded. "Being here with you is what I need."

"Stay as long as you need to."

"Be careful," he joked. How crazy was it he felt like doing that when a few minutes ago he'd been on the verge of an anxiety attack? But Hope was the reason he felt better. "You might not be able to get rid of me."

Josh's eyes dropped to her lips. The urge to kiss her was growing by the second. Except he wasn't here for that. He needed her support, not a kiss or anything else, even if he might want that.

He scooted away. Not far, but enough distance to slow his pulse and lessen the effect of her warmth.

She angled her body toward him, but kept space between them, somehow knowing it was what he needed. "Tell me more about tonight."

He groaned. Maybe she didn't know what he needed because talking wasn't it. "I told you already."

"Tell me again," she encouraged. She'd always seemed strong to him but never like now where an inner strength shined inside her for him to see. It captivated and scared him at the same time. "Talk it out so you feel only pride, not shame or embarrassment."

He nearly rolled his eyes, but Hope didn't deserve that. "You sound like my sponsor or my therapist."

She shot him a mischievous glance. "Is that good or bad? Before you answer, remember you're the one who came to me."

He half-laughed. "I'm not sure what it is, to be honest, but I'd rather be talking to you than anyone else, even if I wish the subject were different and we were dancing on the beach again."

A big smile lit up her face, taking his breath away. "Maybe after talking, we can do something fun. Your leg must be tired. We can relax and watch a movie."

"I want to spend time with you tonight." He kicked off his shoes. "I don't care what we do."

She held his hand. "So talk."

Josh did. This time he added how nervous he was to see her tonight, even though he knew she accepted him for who he was. That seemed to please her. He repeated what he'd done after leaving the reception, going more in depth about his walk and what happened when he went into the bar. He left out no detail, and something interesting happened. The more he told Hope, the better he felt. Those icky, I'm-a-loser feelings lessened. He kept talking, and Hope kept listening. Laughter, a few tears, half-a-dozen cookies, and then yawns…

14

Oh, boy. Hope's back ached. Falling asleep on the couch had not been a good idea. Only she wasn't alone. Her head rested on something warm. A thump-thump sounded in her ear. She blinked open her eyes.

Light streamed through the floor-to-ceiling windows in the living room. She was on the couch curled against Josh. The even sound of his breathing kept her pulse from accelerating into the danger zone. He looked so young and carefree with his eyes closed and the edges of his mouth curved slightly.

Was he having a good dream?

Josh deserved one.

Tentatively, she brushed the hair away from his eyes. The strands were soft against her fingertips when last night everything about him had been hard lines and edges. The devastation written on his face had clawed at her heart. Thinking about it now hurt her stomach.

She'd been out of her element, not knowing what to say or do while he was upset with himself. So she'd listened and tried to support him. There may have been more she could have done, but Josh looked better this morning. Okay, he was asleep, but still…

Hope needed to learn more about recovery so she could help Josh. She wanted him in her life. That much had been clear to her when he'd said she was the one he wanted to be with last night.

I told him I had a place to go, someone to be with who would listen and help me. You.

His words had nestled deep in her heart. He was there, too. She hadn't planned to fall for him, but it had happened. She'd found someone who was worth risking her heart on.

The realization should have terrified her given what she'd gone through with Adam. Except she wasn't afraid.

For the first time in two years, fear wasn't holding her back. She felt… reborn. A second chance at life was waiting for her.

She stared at Josh, her heart turning to a gooey glob.

At love, too?

Time would tell, but Hope didn't want to run from her feelings, didn't want to erect a stronger wall around her heart, didn't want to argue all the reasons this wouldn't work from the distance to his alcoholism.

Truth was, she had no idea what he was going through—what he'd gone through—or what that meant for the future. Could they pursue a relationship as more than friends? That was the big question, but no matter the consequences, she wanted to see where this could go. Possibly nowhere, but that was okay. At least she'd know. That was better than living with regret.

Josh stirred, moving slightly. She straightened so she wasn't half on top of him. Immediately, she missed his warmth and the feel of him against her.

Josh opened his eyes. "Hey."

He sounded sleepy, but the way his lips slipped into a smile told her today would be a better day.

Kissing him good morning would be easy, but she wasn't that brave. Not yet, but soon. She touched his arm instead. "Sleep well?"

"I'm a little sore from the couch." His voice was sharper, no longer dreamy, but the desire in his eyes heated her blood. "But I like seeing you first thing in the morning."

"Same." Waking up together should have been all kinds of awkward given the only other man she'd woken up next to had been her ex-husband, but there was none of that. For her, at least. He didn't seem bothered. Her new awareness of him, however, heightened. "This should feel weirder, right?"

He nodded. "But it doesn't."

Thank goodness. Hope searched his face for any signs he was still upset with himself. "How are you feeling, other than your back?"

"Better, stronger." His voice matched his words. "Thanks to you."

So much needed to be said about what she was feeling. She wanted to know his thoughts and wants, and what they would do about what was between them. But she couldn't organize her jumbled thoughts into something cohesive. She settled on two words. "You're welcome."

Maybe Hope's lack of knowledge about sobriety made her views about his drinking idealistic. Still, she knew the man who showed up at her door last night wasn't a failure. Josh might have viewed himself as one, but she saw him as a man doing his best. His struggles might never go away, but he was trying. She couldn't ask for anything more than that from him.

And wouldn't.

"Are you hungry?" she asked.

"I could eat."

Hope liked being able to do something for Josh after all he'd done for her. "Pancakes sound good?"

"Perfect." He rose. "I'm going to use the bathroom, and then I'll set the table."

As she stirred the batter, she was struck by how normal this morning felt. How was that possible? She'd only known Josh since Tuesday. What had Paula said?

Quality over quantity.

When he returned, she showed him where the

plates were, and he set to work. When he moved behind her, his hand brushed her back. Her insides thrummed like a finely tuned violin.

His smile zinged straight to her heart. "They smell good."

"My grandmother's recipe."

Hope hadn't made breakfast for another man but her brother in two years. Josh didn't offer to take over like Von always did. Or tell her she would burn her hand if she weren't careful like Adam.

"The real secret to good pancakes or waffles, however, is real maple syrup, not the stuff made with corn syrup." She poured the batter onto the griddle. "It's in the fridge along with the butter."

Josh put both on the table along with a bottle of orange juice. That reminded her—he wasn't a coffee drinker. Hope didn't need to brew a pot. She could survive without a cup as long as he was here.

She flipped the pancakes. A few minutes later, she had a stack ready to eat and carried the plate to the table where Josh sat.

"I could get used to this." He placed a napkin on his lap.

Hope slid into the chair across from him. "Having breakfast?"

"With you."

The last remaining piece clicked into place. Being with Josh like this was right. He hadn't said anything about how he felt about her, but the affection in his gaze was clear. Sunday wouldn't be goodbye. This was the beginning of seeing what they might be together.

Joy overflowed. "Me, too, with you."

They ate in comfortable silence.

He added another pancake to his plate. "Man, these are delicious. Addictive like…"

The fork fell from his hand, clattering against his plate. His face paled before scrunching into a look of horror.

The sudden change in him chilled her to the bone. "Josh?"

He pushed back from the table. "I-I have to go."

"Back to the cottage?" She had no idea what was going on.

"Home to Berry Lake." His voice sounded raw like last night, only he looked worse. Like he'd woken up from a nightmare. "This was a mistake. I can't be here with you. Not like this."

His words slammed into her like a runaway train.

No, this wasn't happening. Not when she was finally ready to move on and wanted more with him. When everything he'd done told her he wanted the same thing. Everything had seemed… perfect.

Panicked, Hope jumped to her feet, her chair crashing to the floor behind her. She wouldn't let him go. "Why not?"

Her heart cried out, and she fought for control. He was too important to let walk out of her life. She couldn't when he'd come to mean so much to her.

She rushed around the table to get close to him. He had to feel the connection between them. Each touch had heated her skin. "Tell me what's going on."

* * *

On his knees, Josh ignored Hope while he searched under the sofa for his left shoe. He focused on that because he couldn't leave without it, and thinking about something other than the hurt on her face would keep him from losing it.

"Talk to me," Hope pleaded.

The confusion in her voice cut into him.

"I…" He saw his shoe, grabbed it, and then stood. "I like you, Hope."

"I like you, too."

Hearing those words didn't make him feel better. He hadn't realized what he was doing until eating breakfast this morning and saying the word *addicted*. A warning sound had blared in his brain.

A wake-up call to something he'd been blind to. Or maybe he hadn't wanted to see it.

He'd been warned against this—against starting a relationship—repeatedly. But that was what he'd done. Relationship, romance, whatever one wanted to call it.

All his feelings for Hope, the rush he got being around her, how he felt whole being with her…

This was more than friendship, and he wanted her badly. He needed her like he needed air to breathe and water to drink. Only he couldn't trust if his feelings were real. He couldn't trust anything, especially himself.

"This isn't your fault. I screwed up." He'd known the rules. Sam had even mentioned this to him on Tuesday, but Josh hadn't let that stop his growing feelings and attachment to Hope. He combed his fingers through his hair. "I'm not supposed to date or start a new relationship during the first twelve months of rehab."

"I didn't know that, but we live on opposite sides of the country and won't be seeing each other for a while."

"True, but I…"

No matter what he said, he would hurt her like her ex-husband had. That was killing Josh when her trust in him was as clear as the lips, eyes, and nose on her face. But he couldn't hold anything back. That wouldn't be fair to her.

"You've been kind and understanding." He wasn't sure where the words were coming from or if they were the right ones, but he owed her an explanation. "My sweet angel, my Hope, but since meeting you, I've been lying to myself, to everyone."

Lines creased her forehead. "Lying about what?"

"You."

She flinched. "I don't understand."

Josh wanted to kiss her confusion away, but he forced himself to put on his shoes instead. He had to leave. "We haven't known each other long, but I'm falling for you. Hard."

Her eyes danced, the gold flecks like flames of confetti, and a smile returned to her face. "I feel the same way about you. So what's the problem?"

Josh needed her to understand why their feelings weren't enough. He took a breath and another.

"Part of my recovery has made me look at myself. I don't like what I found." He dragged in yet another breath, letting it out on a shaky exhale. "People have made my life easy because I could throw a football and scramble for yardage. So easy I became a spoiled, entitled brat. I wasn't an adult, but a man-child, an arrogant jerk only looking out for himself."

Maybe that was why he'd enjoyed the 'making amends' step so much. It wasn't only a way to show others he'd changed, but also himself.

"I may have thought my injury pushed me into alcoholism, but I'd been on that path long before I got hurt. I no longer want to be that guy."

"You're not."

"I'm a work in progress."

"I'm willing to wait."

The emotion in her voice made him want to sink to his knees and beg forgiveness. He wanted to ask her to wait, but he couldn't because he had no idea if or when he'd be the man he wanted to be. He wouldn't hold her back like that.

"Go home. You need time. I get that." Her voice

was calm and soothing. "But we can still get to know each other better in the meantime. That's one of the beauties of technology."

If only they could, but he'd never been a do-things-in-moderation kind of guy. It was cold turkey or nothing. That was how he quit drinking. That was the only way to get over these feelings for her—ones he didn't understand nor trust.

"I can't." He forced himself not to touch Hope. If he did, he might not ever let go.

Yes, he was being selfish by not giving her a choice in his decision and hurting her, but at the same time, letting her go wouldn't be easy for him. He wanted her. Needed her. But if he held on the way he wanted, he'd never know if what he felt was real or a substitute for his first love—alcohol. Hope deserved more.

"The way you make me feel is incredible," he added. "Being with you has been wonderful, but I'm afraid you could easily become another addiction. Something I need to function rather than a beautiful addition to my life. If you aren't already."

Pain flashed in her eyes, but it was gone in an instant, replaced by a vacant look that crushed him. Her features went slack. "I, uh, didn't understand. I know little about recovery or what you're going through."

"Don't blame yourself." He didn't want her to make excuses or feel bad that she hadn't known. "You were great last night. What I needed. I wish things could be different, but I'm still finding my way."

She stared down her nose. "But…"

"I can't chance anything right now. A relationship would be a huge risk, especially when I've been warned against it." Saying the words deflated him, even if he knew that was what he needed to do for himself. He only hoped she would forgive him. "It's my choice to stay sober or to drink. No one else's. But I need to limit distractions and regain my focus. If I relapse…"

"I know you don't want to relapse. I don't want that, either." The words flew rapid fire from her mouth. "Do whatever it takes to stay sober."

"Even if it hurts you?"

"Even then," she said without missing a beat. "I care what happens to you, Josh. I want only the best for you. Sobriety. You have my support."

Her selfless words were killing him, and he was reminded again how he didn't deserve her. Josh blinked back tears.

"None of this is your fault. All of it's on me. But you're paying the price for my mistakes." His voice cracked. "Being with you here in Indigo Bay has given me such a sense of peace, a way I haven't felt in a long time, but going into that bar to help Dare's sister reminded me there's no safe place for an alcoholic. The demon is always in reach, always waiting for one more chance to take hold."

Her lower lip quivered. If he hadn't been staring at her so intently, he would have missed it.

Josh couldn't take seeing her pain any longer. He hugged her, burying his face against her hair, smelling her sweet strawberry scent. "I'm sorry. I keep talking about what I need to do, but I'm thinking of you, too. It's better to cause a little hurt now than risk shattering your heart later if I drink again. You deserve more."

She squeezed him before stepping away. "I understand."

He wanted to hold her again. Even now, he didn't want to let go. She had to be the one.

Hope took a breath. "Focus on yourself, staying sober, and being healthy. Forget everything and everyone else, including me."

His breath hitched. She was giving him an out, full permission to do what he needed to do, without a thought to herself. "I won't ever forget you."

"You have to."

Josh hated this was happening. He wanted to be stronger, so he didn't have to hurt someone so caring, but he wasn't there yet. He didn't know if he ever would be. "I wish it could be different."

Her gaze locked on his. In the depths, he saw the truth. She might be telling him to go, but she wanted him to stay.

Josh didn't know how long they stood staring at each other. He never wanted the moment to end.

Hope glanced away, breaking the contact, the

connection. "Life doesn't always turn out as we wished it would, but there's usually a lesson to be learned from that."

"Please don't hate me." The words came out an anguished cry.

She touched his cheek. "I could never hate you."

He leaned into her hand.

Hope lowered her arm before grabbing her phone from the coffee table. "I don't want to be a distraction for you. I'm going to delete you from my contacts. I want you to do the same."

Disappointment sat like a boulder in his stomach. What she suggested needed to be done. A total break. No contact. But hearing her say those words slashed his heart in two.

"The twelve months might be a guideline," she continued, but he wasn't sure if she was talking to him or herself. "Every person is different. This way, neither of us is tempted to reach out. Get your phone."

He did.

Hope's index finger trembled, but that didn't keep her from pressing on the screen. "Done. Your turn."

Josh blew out a breath, raising a finger that felt as if it weighed a ton, and then deleted her info. "Done."

Eyes gleaming, Hope blinked. "Do you need a ride back?

"I'm good."

Leaving was the last thing he wanted to do. He'd rather hold her, kiss her, stay by her side forever. That told him he needed to get away from her.

Josh stood. "Thanks for everything."

"You're welcome." She wrapped her arms around her stomach. Her breaths came faster. "This is for the best."

"The best," he repeated, when all he wanted was a do-over.

"No regrets, okay?"

"No regrets." He hoped that wouldn't turn into a lie once he was back in Berry Lake.

Hope followed him toward the door, but her normal warmth had vanished. She seemed stiff, distant, even though they were less than two feet away from each other.

"Sometimes doing the right thing is hard." She opened the front door. "You'll get through this, Josh. Come out stronger."

"I'm counting on that." His throat burned. Each breath took effort. If he weren't careful, he would cry. He had no idea if she felt the same awful ache in her chest as he did, but she was being too nice when he was the one leaving. "Goodbye, Hope."

"Bye, Josh." She stepped back, making a hug impossible. Probably better this way. "Have a safe flight home."

"Always."

With that, he stepped onto the front porch. The door closed behind him.

As he put one foot in front of the other, forcing

himself away from her and toward his cottage, four words swirled around his head.

It's for the best.

Yes, Hope was correct about that, but that didn't stop the stinging in his eyes or the loneliness threatening to engulf him. He couldn't let either get to him. Josh needed to concentrate and do what needed to be done.

He unlocked his phone. Hit a number on his favorites list. "Hey, Rudy. It's Josh. Sorry to call so early, but there's something you need to know."

15

"I did the right thing."

Hope sat on the floor with her back against the front door, repeating the words to herself between sobs. She wrapped her arms around her bent knees. This was better than the fetal position, right? Though she'd been tempted to roll over and try that more than once.

Saying the words aloud didn't take away the ache in her chest or the empty feeling inside her, nor did it convince her what she said was true. She couldn't stop the tears from falling for Josh and for herself.

"I did the right thing." Based on the pauses between each word, she didn't sound too convincing.

Why did it have to hurt so much?

Somehow in front of Josh, she'd remained in control. Hope wasn't sure how that happened because she'd been ready to break down, but she was grateful she'd held herself together.

He'd been on the verge of tears, which had only added to her heartbreak. If she had cried, she wasn't sure what would have happened. Not losing it had taken every bit of her strength, but the less emotional the goodbye, the better for Josh with a long flight ahead of him and his continued journey to sobriety.

As for her…

Watching him leave was impossible to do without crying. She'd shut the door before letting the tears fall. She wasn't sure if she'd been sitting here for fifteen minutes or five hours. All she knew was Josh Cooper had left. She hadn't known him long, but that hadn't mattered to her heart.

It had only been a few days, but she'd fallen for him. Was it love? Until he'd said he was leaving, she hadn't been sure, but now…

I love him.

But her love equaled another addiction to him.

Well, a possible one as he saw it.

Josh might as well have taken a knife and stabbed her heart after saying what he did. The effect would have been the same.

Her love was too dangerous for him.

Because of that, she'd done what was best for Josh, even if that meant losing him forever.

I miss him already.

Why had she risked her heart again?

He had been worth it. And so was she.

Somehow, she needed to remember that when all she wanted was to beat herself up for allowing her feelings to get out of control.

She rubbed her sore, wet eyes.

Josh's well-being was the most important thing. Hope would do anything to help him. He was the one who had to decide to remain sober. More than anything, she wanted him to move forward and pursue his dreams, whether they were in the broadcast booth, the sky, or somewhere else.

"I did the right thing."

Not being a part of each other's lives was the best for Josh. Logically, she knew that, but her heart wasn't there yet.

Hope wiped the tears from her cheeks. Von would be home for dinner tonight. She didn't want him to see her like this. Or, worse, give him another reason to say 'I told you so'.

You did the right thing.

She rose from the floor, making sure to lock the front door. A shower might help, and then she'd have to see what else could take away the emptiness inside.

* * *

Back in Berry Lake, Josh talked to his family and Dr. Kettering about Hope. They'd been understanding and forgiving about his not mentioning her while he'd been away. More than he'd been with himself, but he was working on that. Rudy had told him to keep showing up for himself, but Hope's words kept him going.

Focus on yourself, staying sober, and being healthy. Forget everything and everyone else, including me.

Josh was trying, except no one else would let him forget about Hope, especially his brother.

"Don't be a jerk," Sam said a week later when he'd called on Sunday morning. He hadn't made it to Berry Lake for the weekend as planned. "I just asked if you'd heard from Hope."

"The answer is the same as it was three days ago. I haven't." Josh sat in his parents' backyard under a clear blue sky. "We deleted each other's numbers from our contacts."

From his earliest sessions with Dr. Kettering, she'd warned him why relationships the first year of recovery were a bad idea. That was why he'd understood how a new addiction could take the place of alcohol, and what he feared was happening with Hope. But that hadn't stopped him from wanting to learn more about the chemistry of love since he'd been home. If only to prove that five days wasn't long enough to fall for someone. That what he'd felt for Hope was nothing more than chemicals causing the same reactions in his brain as drinking had.

"It's for the best," Josh repeated what Hope had told him.

"You sound certain."

"I am." Even if thoughts of Hope struck him at random times. "I've been home longer than I was with her. That's made me wonder what my real feelings for her were."

"Distance and time will make that clearer."

"You think, oh wise one?" Josh teased.

"Hey, I may be younger, but some of the stuff I see during calls makes me feel ancient." Sam sounded off.

"Rough night?" Josh asked, not used to hearing his brother like this.

"One of the worst."

Yet, Sam had called as he said he would. The youngest brother had gotten all the responsible, nice-guy genes in the family. Only Sam had been silent about his life in Seattle, sharing only a funny anecdote or two. Nothing about his job, which must suck at times. Maybe all the time.

Guilt sliced through Josh. His brother was trying to protect him. He couldn't be angry, per se, but he wanted to be part of the family—not the one everyone worried about and watched over. "Seattle's a big city. Move back to Berry Lake. I bet the sheriff would love to hire an officer with your experience."

"I'd die of boredom."

"Boredom might be better than working one rough night after another." Josh took a breath. Something niggled at him. He had to ask. "Are you drinking?"

Sam swore. "After what you've gone through? No, man. I'm not drinking other than one beer if I'm out with the guys. I'm not self-medicating, either, if that's your next question."

"It was."

"Now you sound like an older brother." Sam's tone was skeptical.

"I am older, though I haven't acted like it."

"You've apologized for that. Just stay the course."

The love in Sam's voice hit Josh hard. He'd been a lousy brother and son. Sam was the baby of the family, but Josh had assumed the role. Their parents loved all three of their children but had allowed him to become a golden child diva.

How much had that hurt Ava and Sam? Josh didn't want to know the answer. Not yet anyway. "I will."

The line went quiet.

"And bro?" Sam asked finally.

His brother's tone left a sinking feeling in Josh's stomach. "Do I want to know?"

"Probably not." Sam laughed, but not the carefree sound Josh had grown up hearing. "But I'll say it anyway. Try not to break any more hearts until you hit your twelve-month mark."

"I won't." Josh meant that. He doubted he'd ever find another woman as wonderful or as perfect for him as Hope Ryan.

* * *

June passed slowly, the long, hot days taking forever to turn from one to the next. Hope kept herself busy making items to sell at the various shops in town and favors for events. Cami and Dan's painting remained in the closet, but Hope had done more research about restoring it.

Progress, yes, but she wasn't ready to put the canvas on an easel and try.

Still, she felt off, as if a piece of her was missing and she had no way to get it back.

Von worried about her, but his relationship with Marley was getting more serious, and he wasn't around much. Hope kept telling him she was fine. Maybe not one hundred percent. After a few days of moping, she didn't want to do that any longer. She believed Josh was making progress toward his one-year sober mark and happy where he was. That was enough for her.

July arrived with an explosion of red, white, and blue. Hope loved the patriotic decorations on storefronts and lampposts, but she wasn't sad the next week to see Indigo Bay return to its typical summer vacation crowds instead of bursting at the seams with additional visitors.

In her studio, Hope painted sand dollars—favors for a wedding at the end of the month. Lines from a romantic poem would go on the back, along with the bride and groom's name and wedding date.

Rave reviews about Zoe's beach-themed weddings meant every weekend from now through Labor Day was booked. Most were ordering customized favors from Hope, too. She'd never had so much work.

A knock sounded on the French doors. She looked over to see Paula standing on the deck with a pink bakery box in her hands. Her neighbor must have seen Hope working and bypassed the front door for the direct entrance to the studio.

Hope opened the doors. "What's going on?"

"I've been experimenting with new flavors. I brought you a few samples." Stepping inside the studio, Paula handed over the box. "How are you doing?"

"Pretty good,"

"Come on." Paula's smile spread to her blue-gray eyes. "You're doing better than that."

Hope set the box on her workbench. "What do you mean?"

"When you came back from New York, you were a mess. Not for a week or two, but months. Von and I thought we might have to do an intervention."

She sighed. That had been an awful time, but... "I wasn't that bad."

"You were." Paula gave her a sorry-not-sorry look. "But you had your reasons."

Hope had. "I wanted to divorce Adam, knew in my heart that was the right thing to do, but the way he destroyed the loft and my paintings, then blamed me, he ripped away my power and control of the situation. I felt helpless. Maybe that's why I lost it so badly."

"Do you think not knowing Josh for long helped you not shut down this time?"

"I…" Hope paused, considering. "Call it love at first sight. I had strong feelings for him. It was different from breaking up with Adam, though."

"In what way?"

She remembered the day Josh left. "I had no choice. He needed to put himself first, and I understood that, but it hurt so badly. Still, no matter how I felt or might have wanted things to be different, saying goodbye to Josh was the right thing to do. I miss him, but…"

"What?"

So many things with Josh had been different compared to others. Not only Adam. Von treated her as if she might break. Others believed the rumors and thought she was a crazy person about to go berserk.

Not Josh.

He'd come to her aid in the multipurpose room and by flying her to Nashville, but he'd also seen her as a strong and confident woman. He'd trusted her to be there to help him. She hadn't gotten scared or run away or fallen apart. She'd been the woman he knew she was, the woman she wanted to be and would continue to be.

Not for him or anyone else.

But for herself.

Suddenly what she wanted crystalized in her mind.

She wanted a man who saw her as Josh had, who would recognize her strengths and accept her as she was. The way she'd done with him, too.

"I don't want to close my heart off again. Don't want to say no to a future relationship as I did after Adam." Saying the words loosened the knots inside her. "I want love. I wanted that with Josh, but now I plan to give myself time to heal and hold on to the hope I'll find love down the road."

Paula hugged her. "You will. I know you will."

"Thanks, but I'm in no rush."

"When you least expect it…"

They both laughed.

Hope eyed Paula's dress. "Looks like you're going out with your man."

She nodded. "Dinner, but I wanted to drop off the cake."

"Mission accomplished." Hope shooed her friend toward the door. "Go have fun. I'll get back to work."

As Paula let herself out, Hope squeezed blue paint from the tube and added a dollop of white. The resulting color was a stunning blue.

Like Josh's eyes.

The thought didn't sting. If anything, it comforted her. As would the cake samples after dinner.

Dipping her brush into the paint, she kept thinking of him. Every line and curve of his face was etched into her brain. Her fingers itched for a pencil and a canvas—in a way they hadn't in two years. She wanted to draw Josh. Paint him.

And would.

"Sis?"

That sounded like Von, but he was working in Charleston. Wasn't he?

As if waking from a trance, Hope blinked. Once. Twice...

She was standing in front of a piece of paper on an easel with a paintbrush in her hand. The paper wasn't blank.

Von hugged her from behind. "You're painting."

Staring at the watercolor seascape, Hope leaned back against her brother's chest. Tall, blowing grass surrounded a cherry-red cottage. A football lay hidden in the grass, bottles were half buried in the sand, and a man faced the ocean.

"I don't know what happened." Hope had no idea how long she'd been working. "I was painting wedding favors, and then I wanted to...try."

"You did more than try." Von squeezed her. "You finished, and it's incredible."

"Thanks." And she knew the reason why. Tears stung her eyes.

Josh.

This watercolor was his journey. The man with his back to her was him, and he'd passed all the things he'd left behind. All except...

And then she saw it.

A heart-shaped ornament from Jenny and Dare's wedding hidden toward the back. Hope was there, along with his football career and alcohol.

"You're going to get through this." Von let go of her, moving around to study the canvas. "You'll be okay."

"I know." And Hope did.

Josh Cooper had not only opened her heart to love, but also inspired her to paint. Something she never thought she'd be able to do again.

Thank you.

Working on this painting—albeit in a daze—was giving her something else, something unexpected.

This work had eased the dull ache in her heart. Her breath flowed easier. Her muscles loosened.

Somehow, her subconscious had used Josh as inspiration to open her up again.

"I need to go shopping. Have to buy supplies. I'm ready to paint again."

Von grinned. "Everything that wasn't destroyed from your studio in New York is in boxes in the garage, though some of it may be bad by now."

"You kept the stuff?"

Affection and pride shone in his gaze. "You believed you'd never paint again, but I knew you would."

Maybe twins did have a different kind of connection. "Thanks."

"You'd have done the same for me."

She could never repay Von for all he'd done for her. Not that he wanted anything, but she hoped she would one day get the chance to return the favor. "Love you."

"Love you, sis."

Hope stared at the painting with pride. She'd given up her power to Adam, including her power to paint, but thanks to Josh, she was taking it back.

All of it.

Being able to finish this painting meant everything to her, but it wasn't hers to keep or sell. The watercolor belonged to Josh. They'd agreed not to contact each other, but she'd find a way to deliver it to him. That was the least she could do after all he'd given to her.

* * *

"Welcome back." In Jenny's living room, Josh hugged her and shook Dare's hand. "How was the honeymoon?"

"Amazing." Jenny's normally pale skin glowed with a golden tan. "The resort is all-inclusive. We were spoiled. It was a magical time."

Nodding, Dare slipped his arm around his wife. A fluffy white cat wove between his feet, rubbing against his leg "It was my first time in the Caribbean, but I'd go back in a heartbeat."

Jenny smiled at Dare. "Now that you're out of the army, we'll have plenty of time to travel."

"In between your book deadlines, you mean," Dare joked.

Josh laughed. "You're officially a civilian?"

Dare nodded. "We stopped off in Columbus to finish up the paperwork and have my things shipped. Never thought I'd be happy with a medical discharge, but things didn't heal right after the accident. I'm not able to go back into the field again."

"I understand."

"Sorry, dude." Dare's gaze darkened. "I forgot you, of all people, would know."

Josh nodded.

"Your twelve months has passed, right?" Jenny thankfully changed the subject.

"Yes." He pulled out his coin. "I finally got this."

"We have something else for you." Jenny pulled out a large, flat box tied with a blue ribbon. "Here you go."

Josh stared at the package. "Thanks."

"Aren't you going to open it?" Jenny asked.

Dare shook his head. "That means you should open the gift now or she might."

That made Josh laugh. These two were meant to be together. After pushing off the ribbon, he removed the lid to find white tissue paper. He pulled back the first piece, and then the second.

A matted watercolor painting was inside.

As he peered closer, his pulse raced. In the corner were the initials HR. Hope Ryan? He hadn't spoken to her or stalked her on social media. Once they'd said goodbye, he'd cut her out of his life—deleting her old texts and photos of her from their day sightseeing—to focus on his recovery as she'd wanted him to do and as he'd needed to do.

He'd never seen a watercolor of hers, but... "Where did you get this?"

"Indigo Bay."

He struggled to breathe. "Is it from—"

Jenny held her hands up, stopping him. "It's to mark your twelve months. That's all I can say."

"Sorry, dude," Dare said. "I knew nothing about this, but trust me. If that's all Jenny can say, nothing will drag more out of her."

"Fine." Josh wouldn't put Jenny on the spot. "I'll let it go, but thank you."

Dare pointed near the bottom of the painting. "Hey, look at the football."

Tall grass on the dunes hid the ball. Josh's gaze followed the footprints in the sand leading to half-buried bottles. His breath caught, but he kept following the prints until he came to a heart-shaped ornament. He dragged his gaze back to the footprints of the lone figure, a man who wore clothes like his own, facing the water. Far off on the horizon was a plane—his jet—flying off into the sunset.

He felt a pang in his heart.

All the things he'd left behind—football, alcohol, Hope—on the way to his future. Talk about bittersweet, but he would cherish this forever.

Wait a minute. He studied the watercolor. This picture meant Hope was painting again.

Finally.

His eyes stung. His vision blurred.

Jenny touched his shoulder. "You okay?"

Knowing whatever he said would come out a garbled mess, he nodded.

"You'll need a frame for it," Jenny said. "Sal at the gallery can help you with that."

Another nod.

Jenny sighed. "It's a lovely painting."

"You deserve it," Dare said.

Josh didn't, but he was working hard to be the man who would someday.

"Thanks." He got the word out without embarrassing himself, so he kept going. "It's great seeing you. I want to hear more about your honeymoon, but I have to go now."

Jenny smiled. "We can meet for cupcakes later in the week."

He put the lid on the box before picking it up. "Text me when you and Dare are free, and we'll make it happen."

As Josh headed to his car, he tried not to clutch the box to his chest.

Hope.

She'd said she didn't hate him, and this watercolor was proof of that. He was overcome with a sense of gratitude and giddiness. A way he wasn't used to feeling.

Josh laughed, liking the sound and himself.

She had the perfect name because that was what she'd given him. Back in Indigo Bay and today.

He just had to figure out what to do next.

16

"The exhibition game isn't until this weekend." The concern in his mother's voice matched her gaze, but Josh wasn't about to feel guilty. Not this time. "There's no reason for you to fly out early, honey," she added.

Josh understood why his parents and siblings worried about every decision he made given his past mistakes, but this was something he had to do. "I'm not going to Atlanta right away."

Her laugh lines deepened with her confusion. "Where are you going?"

"Indigo Bay." He wouldn't lie. "I spoke with Dr. Kettering during our last session. She agreed I needed to speak with Hope."

His therapist had offered to roleplay what he wanted to say, but he'd said no to that because he wasn't sure yet. Instead, Dr. Kettering had asked him one question after another until his head wanted to explode.

What if she doesn't want to talk to you?

A few people hadn't when I was in the amends portion of recovery, but that never made me want to drink.

What if she's moved on?

If she's moved on and is happy, I'll be okay with that. Will I be disappointed and hurt? Yes, but I'm the one who left. We agreed not to contact each other, but that was for my benefit, not hers. I could've called her after I hit my twelve-month mark, but I chose not to.

Do you feel bad about not contacting her?

No, because I wasn't ready to talk to her yet.

But you are now?

Yes. I didn't trust myself before, but I'm doing better. No matter what happens, I feel strong enough to get through it without needing a drink. Or ten.

"A lot can change in two months," his mother said.

Josh had changed. For the better. He still had a long way to go, but he was making his own decisions and trusting the outcome. "I have no expectations. I'll be okay."

His mom hugged him. "I hope so. This will either be the closure you need or a new beginning. Either way, it's another step toward healing."

* * *

The next morning, Josh saved a list of meeting times in the Indigo Bay area on his phone, filed a flight plan to Charleston, and then took off.

He had hours on his own to figure out what he wanted to say. "Plenty of time."

Or so he thought.

Now that he was sitting outside Hope's house with the rental car's air conditioning blasting—August was hotter than June had been—he still hadn't a clue, but he had a vague idea and something to give her that he'd bought two weeks ago in New York if their talk went well. He pulled the key from the ignition, walked to the front porch, and knocked.

What they'd shared during those few days in June had been more than a moment in time never to be repeated. Josh hoped she agreed because the memories would never be enough for him.

The door opened. Von squared his shoulders. "What are you doing here?"

Josh had a sense of déjà vu from when he'd visited Jenny in May. That had gone better than he expected. Maybe this would, too. "I want to see Hope."

Von's hard gaze pinned Josh. Hope's brother might be shorter and weigh less, but he didn't back down. He centered himself in the doorway, blocking the way.

"Does Hope know you're coming?" Von asked.

"No." Josh dragged his hand through his hair. "I... I need to see her again. Please."

"Are you sober?"

"Yes." The word burst from Josh's mouth. The good days outnumbered the bad ones by far. He was back at work. But something was missing, and he'd finally figured out what that was. "I received my twelve-month coin in July, but I wasn't ready to come then. She sent me a painting, but I needed more time. Is she doing well?"

"Yes."

Josh breathed a sigh of relief.

"Hope's been painting for the past month." Von sounded hesitant like he wasn't sure what to say to Josh. "Watercolors and a few oils. It's a good start."

Not good. Amazing. "She must be happy."

Nodding, Von held onto each side of the doorway. His expression was torn. Josh could tell he wasn't sure what to do. "I'm not trying to be a jerk, but not painting these past two years messed her up. She needs that outlet in a way other people need water and air. Now that she's found her art again, I don't want anything to screw it up."

Anything equaled Josh.

"I won't. I never wanted to hurt Hope. I'm sorry I did, but if it's any consolation, saying goodbye hurt me, too." His pulse raced like he was doing a two-minute drill with a playoff berth on the line. "I didn't leave only for myself. I left to protect her. She deserves a future she can trust, and I didn't think I could provide that for her then."

"Yet you're here now."

A pressure built in Josh's chest. He swallowed around the lump in his throat. "Yes."

That was all he could say before talking to Hope.

"My sister is fragile."

Josh stared at her brother in disbelief. "She's the strongest woman I know."

"You didn't know her long." Von sounded defensive.

Josh shook his head. "You've known her your whole life, and you have no idea what she's like."

"That's not true."

"Did you know your sister flew to Nashville to pick up a painting she'd done? The couple had bought five of her pieces. All but one was destroyed in a house fire. They asked her to restore it, and out of the kindness of her heart, she agreed even though she hadn't painted in two years."

"I knew she was going."

"Did you know she comforted the couple, hiding her own pain that some of her cherished artwork was gone forever?"

Von wouldn't meet his gaze.

"You make fun of how she earns a living without knowing how painstakingly she creates each favor. How she prepares for every event with the same energy and care she would for her own, simply because she finds her own happiness by making each couple's wedding day dreams come true."

"I was joking."

"You sure about that?"

Von's face reddened. "She knows I'm kidding."

"Did you know she didn't want to let me go, but she did because it was what I needed for my sobriety? Even when she didn't understand my addiction, she accepted me and showed me compassion when I couldn't find any for myself."

Von didn't say anything.

Good… because Josh wasn't finished. "The same as she's done for you, Von. Your sister is strong enough to step out of the way to let you find your own happiness. She never wants to hold you back. Hope feels genuine joy for you and your girlfriend, no matter how lost or heartbroken she might have been. That kind of selflessness takes strength. There's nothing fragile about Hope. Nothing at all."

Von's mouth slanted, but he stepped aside. "If she ends up in tears, I'll hurt you. Bad."

Josh's nerves ramped up. Sweat dripped down his back. But that didn't stop him from crossing the threshold into the house. "If that happens, go ahead because I'll deserve it."

In the studio, Hope washed her hands after taking care of the brushes. She'd been working on restoring Cami and Dan's painting, taking her time to get it right.

So far, so good.

Hope had missed the smell of oil, paint, and turpentine, but having the scents in the studio again was like inviting old friends for a visit. Only, these friends wouldn't be leaving.

She scrubbed her hands, but not all the paint was coming off. Tired, she fought the urge to stretch. That would get water on the floor. She'd been up before the sun, spending time outside sketching various cottages down the road before working on the painting. No sense making more of a mess when it was time to quit for the day.

She was ready to close the door to her studio. Overdoing only led to a sore back, exhaustion, and a worried brother. Because of that, she'd agreed with Von to set a time to work and a time to stop each day. Sometimes she succeeded.

Like today.

That meant a reward.

A piece of berry pie at Sweet Caroline's Cafe sounded good. She would text Paula. See if she could leave work early and meet her. Her friend loved her job but worked too hard.

"Hope."

A shiver shot down her spine. It didn't stop until reaching her toes. Hope didn't have to turn around to know Josh was here. She would recognize his voice anywhere. With a deep breath to calm herself, she shut off the water, dried her hands, and faced him.

He stood in the doorway, wearing cargo shorts, a T-shirt, flip-flops, and a worried expression.

Her pulse kicked up a notch. Okay, three.

Hope raised her chin. She couldn't tell if she was smiling or if her expression looked as stunned as seeing him made her feel. "You came back."

Her voice was barely above a whisper. She hadn't asked a question—or said anything eloquent—but it was the first thing she'd thought to say.

"I have to be in Atlanta this weekend for a game. I thought I'd stop by before flying there."

His words sank in. That meant… "You're back to broadcasting."

"We're doing exhibition games this month. It's good to be in the booth again."

This was what Josh needed to get his life back on track. "Wow. That's great."

He took a closer look at the painting she'd been trying to repair. "Thanks for the watercolor."

"You're welcome." Jenny had told Hope how affected Josh had been by the gift, but she'd never expected him to return to Indigo Bay. "That watercolor got me painting again. It was if a switch was flipped back on. I'm grateful to you for helping me find that missing piece of my life."

His face softened. "We both helped each other."

She nodded.

An awkward silence fell over the studio. She

couldn't allow it to continue. "Things going well for you besides work?"

Josh's shoulders pushed back. "Almost thirteen months sober."

Pride for him rushed through her. "Congrats."

"I never want to drink again, and I'm doing everything I can to make sure I don't. But it'll always be something I have to work at."

A new strength shone in Josh. Not only strength but also understanding. He'd finally accepted himself and his situation. "We made the right decision in June."

"I know." He rubbed the back of his neck. "All I've thought about lately was seeing you again, but now that I'm here the words won't come."

Her gaze on his, she took a step forward but forced herself to stop even though all she wanted to do was comfort him. She still needed to look out for herself. "You don't have to say anything."

"Yes, I do." The longing in his eyes made her want to turn back the calendar to mid-June. "I miss you, Hope."

Her heart lurched. She'd survived his leaving once, but she didn't want to put herself through that again. "Josh…"

"Do you miss me?" The words sounded unsure, a little desperate, so unlike the confident man who had spoken a few seconds ago.

A lump burned in her throat. She swallowed

around it. "Yes, but I don't think—"

"I was wrong." He cut the distance between them in half. "About you. Us."

She wrapped her arms around her stomach. "No, you weren't. I did some research. Learned about neurosciences and addiction. Dopamine pathways—"

"I wasn't trading one addiction for another." He continued toward her. "No matter how hard I tried to tell myself what I felt was due to brain chemistry or another addiction, the feelings were real. But it took me a while to get there. To trust myself about what I felt because I'd never felt this way about anyone before. I was confused. Scared. Needed to figure things out. Work on myself so I'd be good enough for you."

"I don't understand." She stepped back until her backside hit the sink.

"I don't deserve you. I'm not sure I'll ever be in a place where I will. For all my good intentions, there's the chance I may relapse. I'm not a good bet for the future." His gaze remained locked on hers. "But I want you. I've never stopped wanting you."

Her heart thudded. She thought it might explode out of her chest. "I-I…"

"It's your turn not to say anything." As his thumb rubbed along her jawline, a burst of heat rushed through her. "I'm not talking about wanting sex, Hope. I'm talking about wanting you. I haven't seen you in over two months, but my feelings have only gotten stronger. Deeper. I want all of you. Heart, body, and soul. But I don't need you to complete me. I need you to enhance my life. I love you."

She wanted to believe him, but a part of her was scared. "You love me?"

"Yes, I love you."

The words wrapped around her heart like an heirloom quilt, taking away her fear and making her want to risk it all. Especially if that meant him declaring his love over and over again.

"You're intelligent, caring, and the kindest woman I know. I respect you so much. When you saw the good in me, I tried to see it, too. And somewhere along the way of falling in love with you, I learned to love myself." Josh's lips curved into a charming smile meant only for her. "I have a long way to go on this journey, but I want you by my side.

"Oh, Josh. I love you." Laughter bubbled over. She wondered if her feet still touched the floor. "I told myself that was the last thing I wanted, but then I met you. I'm not sure how it happened so fast, but it did. And I wanted to forget all the bad stuff that had happened in the past. When you left, I couldn't stop crying."

Josh cupped her face. "I'm sorry, sweetheart."

"I know, but I also knew saying goodbye was the right thing for you and for me." She leaned into his hand. "You aren't like the others. When most people look at me, they see an artist barely hanging on, trying not to fall apart, but not you. You saw something more.

A strong, capable woman."

"That's what you are."

"It's what I wanted to be, and you helped me realize I was." A sigh welled inside her. "After you left, I spent a few days throwing myself pity parties, but that was all. It still hurt, and I missed you, but I didn't give up. Not like I did with Adam. I couldn't because I wanted to remain strong. For you and for me."

"You're incredible."

He lowered his mouth toward Hope's. His lips pressed against hers.

Soft, caring, *home*.

That was what kissing Josh felt like.

His taste was the same as she remembered, but the sense of urgency she remembered was gone. His lips lingered and caressed as if they had all the time in the world.

He backed away. "I needed that."

Her lips tingled. "Me, too."

Josh hadn't let go of her, and she was thrilled he hadn't. "So many things are keeping us apart— distance, our families, my job, your painting, my sobriety—but I don't care. I want to make this work."

"So do I." A newfound certainty glowed inside her. He was everything she wanted. It wouldn't be easy, but life wasn't meant to be. "I'm not the same woman I was when I got divorced. I can't fix you or save you, but I can love and support you through the good and bad times. The distance now doesn't mean forever, but as long as we have each other, we can do this."

"We'll go slow. Given how we started off, though, that might be a good thing." He brushed his lips over hers. "I won't let anything come between us."

"Neither will I." A kiss was her promise to him.

"I want us to take our time, but I also want you to know I'm committed to you." He removed a pretty blue box from his pocket. "This is for you."

Hope opened the lid. Inside was a fabric pouch of the same color. She pulled out a silver chain.

A solitaire diamond ring hung on the necklace.

Her jaw dropped. "I…"

"I'm serious about wanting more, but we both need time. I'd like to put this around your neck today for you to wear as a sign of my commitment to you. And one day, when we're both ready, I promise to go down on one knee, ask for your hand in marriage, and place the ring on your finger."

"I-I…"

"Is that a yes?"

She nodded, turning her back to him and lifting her hair off her neck.

He undid the clasp, put the necklace on her, and then moved in front of her to arrange it. "There. It fits you perfectly."

"Beautiful."

He stared at her. "Yes, you are."

Heat flooded her face.

"There's the blush I missed." Affection filled his eyes.

"Thank you." Hope rested her head against his chest. She blinked back tears. "This is so much better than any dream."

"It's only the beginning, Hope." He kissed her. "Our new beginning. Wait and see. There's so much more ahead of us."

Epilogue

A year and a half later...

People packed the art gallery in Berry Lake, Washington, including Josh's family, Von, and Hope's parents, who had surprised her earlier at dinner. She was thrilled to have everyone here on the opening night of her exhibit, but that didn't stop her from hiding away in an alcove with a large sculpture standing on a pedestal.

She couldn't decide if the figure was supposed to be a gorilla or Sasquatch. Given the town's love and obsession with Bigfoot, she'd go with the latter.

"Hope you don't mind the company, Squatchy," she said to the statue. "I need a break."

She wiped her sweaty palms on her navy floral-print maxi skirt. The urge to peek around the corner where her paintings hung was strong, but one painting had sold—success! woohoo!—so she forced herself not to look to see if a sold sticker had been added to any more of them.

Not that she'd expected to sell anything tonight. She was stunned to have paintings on display somewhere outside of the gallery in Indigo Bay.

You have to start somewhere.

That was what Josh had said when Sal, the Berry Lake gallery owner, had approached her about selling the pieces she worked on when she visited Berry Lake. Sal had known all about Hope, but her past hadn't deterred him. With Josh's support, she'd said yes.

And here she was. "Trying not to freak out."

At least the statue didn't talk back.

"Hey, I'm usually the one hiding at these things." Jenny O'Rourke pulled Hope out of the alcove. The author wore an empire-waist dress that didn't quite hide her baby bump. "Tonight is not the time to be shy. Go mingle so everyone can tell you how talented you are."

Hope appreciated the words, but she wasn't a hundred percent comfortable here. What happened with Adam was in the past, but a few lingering fears about being featured in a show remained. Josh knew and understood, but others didn't. "I needed a minute."

Jenny grinned. "It's been ten."

That brought a smile. "Spying?"

"Writers have mad observation skills," Jenny

joked. "But Josh asked if I'd seen you. He's worried this is too much for you."

Hope pushed back her shoulders. "I'm still here."

"Hope," Josh called, relief in his voice. "I've been looking for you."

"Glad you found her." Jenny winked. "I'm going to find Dare. See you later."

Josh's blue eyes studied Hope. "You okay?"

She nodded but took a step back toward her new BFF Bigfoot. "Hanging out with Squatchy."

He raised an eyebrow, giving her his tell-the-truth look.

"I told you I would feel weird being here," she admitted.

He pulled her into his arms. She rested her head against his chest.

"And?" he asked.

She sighed, knowing he wouldn't judge her. If anything, he'd make her feel better. "I keep waiting for…"

"Something bad to happen," he finished for her. He brushed his lips over her hair.

"Maybe I am crazy."

"Not crazy. You're an artist having a show. You're allowed to be emotional." As he held her against him, he rubbed her back. As usual, the tension seeped away with each touch of his hands. "But nothing bad will happen. Everyone you love and who loves you is here."

She combed her fingers through his hair the way she knew he liked. "I want to believe that, but only one painting has sold tonight."

"Then the other buyers haven't arrived," he said as if it wasn't a big deal. "You saw Sal's smile when he put that first sold tag on. He's thrilled to feature you. He's salivating to see what you're working on next. So am I."

She put up her hands. "Not until it's finished."

"Something else is bothering you."

Josh knew her so well. Hope might as well tell him. She couldn't keep anything from him. "I don't want to disappoint you."

"Oh, baby." He kissed her. "That isn't going to happen. In case you forgot, I'm the screwed-up one in this relationship."

Things weren't perfect between them, but they were better than Hope imagined they'd be. Josh was sober. She was painting. Life was good.

She kissed him. "You're my muse."

"And you're my Hope." He glanced around. "I was going to do this later tonight, but now seems like the right time."

"What?"

He dropped to his knee. "Hope Ryan, you're everything I didn't know I needed in my life. You're my first thought in the morning. My last one at night. I want to spend every day with you. Will you marry me?"

Her hands covered her mouth. She struggled to breathe. "Oh, oh, yes. I'll marry you."

Josh stood. "I need to take off your necklace."

She'd worn her hair up, so that made it easier. Her heart raced.

He removed the ring and then clasped the chain around her neck again. Good, she'd gotten used to wearing it.

Josh slipped the ring onto her finger. A perfect fit. "I have no idea where this journey will lead us, or where we'll end up living—in Indigo Bay, Berry Lake, or somewhere else—but you're the only one I want by my side as we find out."

Her heart swelled with affection for this imperfect man who was trying his best. "I love you."

"And I love you." He kissed her. "I will always love you, Hope."

* * * * *

I hope you enjoyed **Sweet Beginnings**. I've wanted to write Josh's story ever since I mentioned him in my novella **Jenny** (Jenny and Dare's story) available at melissamcclone.com/jenny. If you want to read about Mitch and Lizzy Hamilton (and get an update on Jenny and Dare), check out my short read **Sweet Holiday Wishes** available at melissamcclone.com/sweet-holiday-wishes.

For those of you dealing with alcoholism, you're not alone. There are organizations to help when you're ready to take that step.

Alcoholics Anonymous: www.aa.org

Ala-non (for families and friends worried about someone with a drinking problem): al-anon.org

WHAT COMES NEXT?

If you're ready to spend more time in Indigo Bay, we have stories for you to read! Here's a list of all the titles in the series. All stories are standalone and can be read in any order.

Spring 2018
Sweet Saturdays (Book 7) by Pamela Kelley
Sweet Beginnings (Book 8) by Melissa McClone
Sweet Starlight (Book 9) by Kay Correll
Sweet Forgiveness (Book 10) by Jean Oram
Sweet Reunion (Book 11) by Stacy Claflin
Sweet Entanglement (Book 12) by Jean C. Gordon

Christmas 2017 Short Reads
Sweet Holiday Memories by Kay Correll
Sweet Holiday Wishes by Melissa McClone
Sweet Holiday Surprise by Jean Oram
Sweet Holiday Memories by Danielle Stewart

Spring 2017
Sweet Dreams (Book 1) by Stacy Claflin
Sweet Matchmaker (Book 2) by Jean Oram
Sweet Sunrise (Book 3) by Kay Correll
Sweet Illusions (Book 4) by Jeanette Lewis
Sweet Regrets (Book 5) by Jennifer Peel
Sweet Rendezvous (Book 6) by Danielle Stewart

You can find a listing of the titles and buy links at our webpage at sweetreadbooks.com/indigo-bay.

ABOUT THE AUTHOR

USA Today bestselling author Melissa McClone has written over forty sweet contemporary romance novels and been nominated for Romance Writers of America's RITA® Award. She lives in the Pacific Northwest with her husband, three children, two spoiled Norwegian Elkhounds, and cats who think they rule the house. If you'd like to learn more about Melissa, please visit her website at www.melissamcclone.com, Facebook page at www.facebook.com/melissamcclonebooks or on Twitter at twitter.com/melissamcclone.

OTHER BOOKS BY MELISSA MCCLONE

Prequels to Sweet Beginnings

Jenny
melissamcclone.com/jenny

Sweet Holiday Wishes
melissamcclone.com/sweet-holiday-wishes

Standalone Romances

Fiancé for the Night
melissamcclone.com/FFTN

Ever After Series
The Honeymoon Prize
melissamcclone.com/THP

The Cinderella Princess
melissamcclone.com/TCP

Christmas in the Castle
melissamcclone.com/CATC